Molly and the
Gold Baron

Molly and the
Gold Baron

Stephen Overholser

Thorndike Press
Waterville, Maine USA

Chivers Press
Bath, England

This Large Print edition is published by Thorndike Press®, USA and by Chivers Press, England.

Published in 2003 in the U.S. by arrangement with Golden West Literary Agency.

Published in 2003 in the U.K. by arrangement with Golden West.

U.S. Hardcover 0-7862-5364-9 (Western Series)
U.K. Hardcover 0-7540-7277-0 (Chivers Large Print)
U.K. Softcover 0-7540-7278-9 (Camden Large Print)

The text of this Large Print edition is unabridged.
Other aspects of the book may vary from the original edition.

Set in 16 pt. Plantin by Al Chase.

Printed in the United States on permanent paper.

British Library Cataloguing-in-Publication Data available

Library of Congress Cataloging-in-Publication Data

Overholser, Stephen.
    Molly and the gold baron / Stephen Overholser.
      p. cm.
    ISBN 0-7862-5364-9 (lg. print : hc : alk. paper)
    1. Owens, Molly (Fictitious character) — Fiction.
    2. Women private investigators — Colorado — Cripple Creek
    — Fiction.   3. Cripple Creek (Colo.) — Fiction.
    4. Gold mines and mining — Fiction.   5. Large type books.
    I. Title.
    PS3565.V43M564 2003
    813'.54—dc21   2003045905

Molly and the
Gold Baron

CHAPTER I

Raising the field glasses to her eyes, Molly brought the posse into focus. A quarter of an hour before the dozen horsebackers had been dark specks leading a cloud of billowing dust. Now, in the valley below her ridgetop position, Molly saw men, and she recognized one squat figure on a roan horse as Joe Sears, U.S. Marshal.

She lay on a flat outcropping of granite and watched the riders follow the trickle of a stream that creased the valley floor. The posse rode past, then slowed and circled back. The man in the lead was hatless, with long, black hair. He was a tracker, Molly realized, and a good one. He'd lost the trail and now was intently searching the ground.

Seeing the tracker lift an arm in her direction, Molly edged back on the sun-warmed rock. She raised to all fours, turned, and crawled away, the field glasses dangling from her neck. She was a lithe woman with full breasts and a slender waist above the curve of her hips, and she dressed like a ranch woman with her blue-denim riding skirt, light cotton blouse, and cowhide boots. Her long blonde hair was pinned up under her Stetson.

She swung down over the far edge of the granite outcropping and dropped to the ground four or five feet below. In the shade there sat Charley Castle, holding the reins of their lathered horses.

"What's Joe up to?" he asked.

"Us," Molly replied. "His tracker figured out where we left the valley."

"Well, damn," Charley said in frustration. He got to his feet, grimacing as he put weight on his right ankle.

Molly moved to her horse. She took off her hat, then pulled the field glasses over her head and shoved them into the leather case hanging from the saddle horn.

"Joe Sears must have an Indian working for him," Charley said, "the way that posse's glued to us."

Molly put on her Stetson. She turned to look at him. Even with several days' growth of beard on his jaw, Charley Castle was a handsome man — as handsome as he was exasperating. He wore a low-crowned straw hat and a cream-colored suit, now soiled

8

and much wrinkled.

"I know what you're thinking, Molly," he said, raising his hands in protest. "You're thinking I dragged you into this, that you never figured on being a fugitive and all that."

"I'm thinking," Molly said, "that you're hurt, the posse is on top of us, and our horses are blown. I'm thinking we should cash it in. You can explain everything in court. You're good at explaining."

Charley shook his head as he moved to his horse. "I wouldn't stand a chance against that setup in Bluebell," he said. "Believe me." He stepped into the saddle and turned his horse.

"Molly, you'd better peel off now," he said, looking down at her. "Joe Sears isn't hunting you. He wants me. And the longer he chases, the madder he gets. By now, he'd just as soon take me in feet first."

Molly pursed her lips in a moment of decision. Last night, she'd agreed to ride out of Denver with him. The deck was stacked against him, and for once in his life, Charley Castle was an innocent man.

Convinced of that and remembering a past debt, Molly knew she had to play this out to the end. As Charley guided his horse past her and started down slope, she thrust

9

her boot into her saddle stirrup and mounted.

At breakneck speed, she followed him straight down the steep slope. The horses stumbled and slid all the way to the bottom, sending a cascade of stones and dirt ahead. They crashed through a stand of willows on the bank of a dry wash, turned, and trotted along the sandy bottom. Ahead, less than a quarter of a mile away, Molly saw a vast pine forest that spread into the widening valley.

She looked around. The surrounding foothills shouldered against the snowy peaks of the Colorado Rockies. Hillsides were scarred by mines and prospect holes, marked by heaps of earth and rock that were oxidized to a rust color by time and weather. She knew that in this maze of valleys and hidden canyons Charley planned to dodge the posse.

They had ridden only two hundred yards when she heard the booming report of a rifle. An instant later, a bullet thudded into the sand nearby. Charley's head snapped around as he looked back the way they had come.

The worn-out horses were spooked into a faster trot. Molly ducked down against her mount's neck. More shots boomed, raising mushrooms of sand all around her.

Charley led the way into the pine forest. Deep in the cool shadows there, he halted his horse and swung down. Molly reined in behind him.

"They'll ride us down," he said, quickly untying his saddlebags. "Let your horse go."

Molly dismounted and grabbed her field glasses and canteen. Slinging them over her shoulder, she moved behind her saddle and took off the saddle bags.

Charley ran behind the horses and slapped their rumps. The animals bolted, galloping away and soon disappearing in the shadows of the trees.

Behind, Molly heard the dozen pursuing horses plowing down the steep ridge she and Charley had just descended. She turned and saw him hobble uphill through the trees and ran after him.

The pine forest ended abruptly at a sheer wall of granite that stretched high overhead, higher than the tree tops. Upon reaching it, Charley fell.

"Charley!" Molly dropped her gear and rushed to him, skidding to her knees.

Charley rolled over on his back. He reached up and grabbed her, pulling her down on top of him.

11

"Shhhhh," he whispered.

Molly clung to him, listening to her own heart pound against his chest. Moments later, she heard horses and the creak of saddle leather, then voices as the posse entered the forest.

"Careful now," came the voice of Marshal Sears. "Ambush, maybe."

Another, slower voice answered, "Horses running — that way."

"All right," Sears said. "Keep after them." Molly heard the posse move rapidly through the trees, and soon men and animals were out of earshot.

"You smell good."

Molly raised up, placing her elbows on Charley's chest. "You don't." Looking into his slate-blue eyes, she saw a mischievous glitter.

"You're the woman of my dreams," he said, sliding his hands underneath her and grasping her breasts. "And now I have you on my bed of pine needles."

"Charley, how can you think of that now?"

"Might be the last time," he said with a faint smile. "Those saloon deputies will chase our horses through the trees for a while, but as soon as they catch one, they'll come back."

"What are we going to do?" she asked.

Charley looked straight up. "I've often wondered how long a man could hide in a tree. Who looks up into trees besides kids and old folks?"

Molly tipped her head back and looked up. The ponderosa pine tree she saw appeared to stretch endlessly skyward. "You're going to climb up there?"

"No, I'm going to run like hell," Charley said, squeezing her breasts. "Get off me."

Molly moved aside and raised to her knees. She watched Charley get to his feet, favoring his right leg.

"How's your ankle?" she asked.

"All right," he replied, picking up his saddlebags.

"Which way are you going to run?" she asked.

"Where that lawman would least expect," Charley said. Glancing at her, he added, "Stay here. I don't want you slowing me down. I mean it."

Molly met his gaze. She recognized this ploy and knew that he now feared for her safety. "Try to lose me, Charley."

"You're a pushy woman, Molly Owens," he said, looking off into the forest. "I just don't understand what civilization's coming to. Here I am, running from a murder I

13

didn't commit, and now all this running and chasing seems like a sad, pointless game —" His voice trailed off, and then he turned and strode away without looking back.

Molly stood and grabbed up her saddlebags, field glasses, and canteen. She followed Charley as he made his way through the pines that grew along the base of the granite wall. He stopped when he reached a wide, jagged crack that divided the cliff all the way to the top.

Charley stepped into this crack, looking up as he ran his fingers along the gray and black speckled granite. Then he slung his saddlebags over his shoulder and lifted his boot to a foothold. He placed his other boot on a higher foothold, groaning with pain as he stepped up.

Molly watched. He climbed slowly, at times pressing his back flat against one side of the crack while moving his feet up the other side, one after the other, then reaching overhead until he found a handhold. Grabbing it, he would pull his body up.

She followed, trying to use the same footholds and handholds Charley had found. The gear she carried hampered her progress and, a dozen feet off the ground, her boot slipped, and she fell.

Molly's fingers slid rapidly down the rock, but she caught a handhold the instant before she lost her balance. Bracing herself with both feet, she shifted the field glasses and canteen from her shoulder and looped them around her neck.

Inching upward, Molly climbed very slowly, never looking down. She was aware that Charley had already reached the top. He was out of sight.

A cooling breeze swept across her face. The air was scented with pine. She stopped for a rest and looked out over the tree tops. Green boughs, swaying in the breeze, were laden with pine cones.

Somewhere down there is the posse, she thought, and began climbing again.

Near the top of the cliff, the crack widened, and the stone slanted away. Climbing now was a matter of crawling up the slanting rock on all fours. Molly was arm and leg weary, her fingers raw from clinging to the rough granite.

Reaching the flat top, Molly straightened up and looked out over the ridge, seeing high peaks of the Rockies in the background. Behind her, this ridge sloped down toward the forest.

Charley was nowhere in sight. Molly drank from her canteen, then stood and carried her gear as she walked along the summit of the ridge, moving up-slope more from intuition than from logic. She heard a distant roar. Hurrying toward the sound, a refreshing smell of water mist came into the pine-scented air. The roar was from a waterfall in the next canyon.

Movement caught her eye. Ahead, fifty yards away, she saw Charley leaning over the precipice of this granite formation that overlooked the canyon. His back was to her, as he was obviously searching for a way down. She hurried on toward him.

The growing noise of the waterfall covered the sounds of horses' hoofs on stone. Molly sensed their presence or perhaps caught the odor of sweating men and horses, and she stopped in midstride, looking back.

With horrifying clarity, she saw Joe Sears and the eleven men of the posse. In their moment of discovery, the men's mouths stretched open, eyes widened, and all of them reached for their guns.

The sight took Molly's breath for an instant, but then she turned and screamed a warning.

Charley raised up and looked around. A rifle boomed, followed by more shots. Straw hat flying off his head, Charley was driven backward by the impact of bullets pounding into his chest. His hands clawed the air as he stumbled back, falling over the side of the precipice.

CHAPTER II

"I hate a knife. God, I hate a knife." The sobbing fat woman lying on the other bunk in the cell brought Molly awake with her muttering.

Sitting up, Molly looked through the bars of the women's cell block in the basement of the Denver City Jail. Dimly illuminated by two smoky lamps out in the corridor between the rows of cells, this musty place stank of coal oil and sweat. The prisoners in the barred cages were never silent. During the night, screams and laughter and sobs made a nightmare vision of hell, where there could be no peace.

The fat woman had either witnessed a knifing the previous night or committed one. Molly didn't know which. Probably, the woman herself didn't know, for she had been prodded into the cell after midnight, raving about a knife and smelling of whiskey and vomit.

All night, she had moaned and muttered,

and her whining voice had seeped into Molly's dreams during snatches of sleep.

Sleep was the escape Molly had sought since she was arrested by Joe Sears and brought to the cell the previous afternoon. The memory of Charley tumbling out of sight was imprinted in her mind. In strange, fragmented dreams, she relived everything that had happened. She again dropped her saddlebags to the ground and ran to the edge of the precipice. She looked over the side. In the canyon bottom, five hundred feet below, was a rushing mountain stream at the base of a waterfall. On a boulder down there sprawled the body of Charley Castle, and floating in an eddy at the edge of the current Molly saw his straw hat, slowly turning.

These vivid recollections dulled her memory of what followed. She had been brought back to Denver by the marshal while his posse entered the canyon far downstream to recover Charley's body.

Molly knew he was dead, but her mind tried to deny it, and in the background of her dreams was the sobbing of a woman, like a reminder of the truth.

Before noon, the stout jailer, a woman with a man's husky voice, came and took Molly upstairs to a detention room. There she was left alone for half an hour until the door swung open and a small, clean-shaven man marched in. He wore a dark suit, a white shirt with a starched collar, and a bowler hat. He carried a black leather briefcase.

"Molly Owens," he said, hefting the briefcase on to the one table in the room. "I am William Cole, your attorney." He glanced at her, then opened the latches of his briefcase with quick, precise movements.

"Attorney," Molly said, hearing a tone of vagueness in her own voice. She realized that she must seem slow to this abrupt little man, but she was groggy from lack of sleep and still felt dazed from the events of yesterday and the experience of being arrested, questioned, and jailed.

"That's right," Cole said. "I have been retained by Mr. Horace J. Fenton of New York City." He cast a disdaining look at her. "I have been advised of your . . . profession."

"How did Mr. Fenton find out I'd been arrested?"

Cole interrupted. "One of your fellow operatives here in Denver heard of your arrest and notified him by telegraph. He, in turn, sent a message to me. If a court appearance became necessary, I was to represent you."

"Court," Molly repeated.

Cole sighed. "Miss Owens, whether you know it or not, you were to be charged with aiding a criminal, possibly a murderer, in eluding a federal marshal."

"If anyone should be charged with a crime," Molly said, her voice rising, "Joe Sears should be. He shot Charley down."

"Now that's another case," Cole said. He reached into his briefcase and pulled out an envelope. He turned and held it out toward her. "My job was to represent you. I've done that by convincing the prosecutor that his case was too weak to stand. You're free to go." He stared at her, obviously expecting praise.

Molly reached out and took the paper from him, making no reply.

"Now if you want to go after a respected lawman like Joe Sears," Cole said, closing up his briefcase, "you'll have to find yourself another attorney. Good day." He snatched his briefcase off the table and strode out of the room, leaving the door standing open behind him.

Molly stared at that open doorway for several moments, realizing from the way he'd said *respected* that he was an admirer of Joe Sears and had little regard for women investigators.

21

Opening the envelope, she pulled out the telegraphed message and read it.

May 22, 1895

Operative Molly Owens:
At your earliest convenience, relay to me the circumstances of your arrest.

Horace J. Fenton, President
Fenton Investigative Agency
New York City, New York

Upstairs in Mrs. Boatwright's Boarding House for Ladies, Molly reclined neck deep in an iron bathtub filled with steaming water. She soaked sore muscles, eyes closed, trying not to remember.

The effort failed. She remembered all too well. The night before his death Charley Castle had stolen a ladder from a carriage house next door to the boarding house, propped it against the outside wall, and climbed to her window.

Awakened by repeated taps on the glass, Molly met him with her revolver in hand. Recognizing him by starlight, she opened the window. Molly was not particularly surprised by a late-night visit from him, but this time she sensed immediately that he was on the run.

Charley came in, quickly explaining in a loud whisper that he had been framed for the murder of a woman in the mining camp of Bluebell, and for the last three days he'd been doing his damnedest to shake a posse led by federal marshal Joe Sears.

Molly listened intently, thinking all the while that although this man had been out of her life for months, he still turned to her for help. Charley Castle was a tumbleweed, a supreme confidence man who was famous for his sleight-of-hand tricks for crowds gathered on street corners and notorious for bilking wealthy investors by selling them salted gold mines or lead bricks plated with gold.

Molly knew all too well of his schemes, having first met him when she'd been assigned to locate him and bring him in for trial. She knew that he was a smooth talker, a liar by trade, but she came to understand why he was grudgingly admired even by those he had swindled. The man lived by his own sense of fair play, claiming always that he only presented opportunities to the greedy. Liar, yes. Murderer, no.

Charley explained that he needed time, and he needed the help of an experienced investigator to prove his innocence. Molly agreed without hesitation. This man had once saved her life. Perhaps such a debt could never be repaid, but she would give him whatever he asked.

He undressed in the darkness of her room while she went to the bathroom at the end of the hall and brought back a bucket of hot water. After a sponge bath, he climbed into bed with her.

"No time for sleep," he said, reaching for her.

Molly felt his hands run over the soft curves of her body. He tugged at the straps of her satin nightgown.

"Take that thing off," he said.

She gathered the gown up over her waist, then sat up and lifted it over her shoulders and head. She gave her hair a shake and sank to the bed under his embrace.

Molly returned his kiss, feeling her own passion mount as he held her against the length of his body. She held him for a long moment, then released him as he began caressing her.

Aroused by the memory of their love-making, Molly now raised her toes out of the soapy water. She stared absently at them while miniature rainbows on soap bubbles slid away, remembering her surging passions as Charley stroked her. She was enormously excited when he gained position over her and she grasped him and guided him into her body. Back and forth, his movements were slow at first, deliciously and tantalizingly slow, then faster and stronger, bringing her desire to a peak at the moment his body lurched against her and his warmth spurted into her. They clung to one another, wet with perspiration, in a passionate embrace. Molly remembered those moments of time that were immeasurable, moments that were at once satisfying and thrilling, moments that were never to be again.

In the darkness before dawn, they had ridden out of Denver on a main road. The road must have been watched, and too late Molly realized that a man in a cream-colored suit was conspicuous. By daybreak, the posse was not far behind, as Sears and his deputies had not been since Charley had leaped out of the second-floor window of the Bluebell Queen, spraining his ankle. The Bluebell Queen was a brothel, and Charley suddenly understood that he had been lured there to be found with a murdered prostitute. One of his pigeons was a poor loser.

That was the hasty explanation Molly heard as they rode into the foothills west of Denver. Charley knew this country and, over his shoulder, assured Molly that he had a plan. But by the time they entered that mountain valley, Molly had seen a cloud of dust on their back trail.

Remembering, she submerged her feet into the water, watching the glistening soap bubbles swirl and delicately explode in the wake. That morning, after she was released from jail, she had gone straight to the telegraph office and wired a reply to her employer.

Molly briefly described the events that led up to her arrest by Marshal Sears. She offered no apologies or regrets to Mr. Fenton, knowing full well that the high standards of his investigative agency left no room for operatives with arrest records. She fully expected to be released from the agency, and while lying in this tub of hot water, she tried to reconcile herself to the inevitable.

Molly had climbed out of the bathtub and was toweling herself dry when she heard a familiar voice outside the door.

"Molly?"

"Yes, Mrs. Boatwright," she replied. "Come in."

The door opened, and the owner of the boarding house entered the steamy bathroom. "A courier was here, Molly, and left this package for you."

Molly recognized the wrapped file folder in the woman's outstretched hand as a packet of background information from the Fenton home office in New York City. Evidently, Mr. Fenton had assigned her to a new case before learning of her arrest. That explained the terse message he'd sent by wire.

"Thank you," Molly said, crossing the room to her robe hanging from a brass hook on the wall. "I'll take it to my room."

Mrs. Boatwright smiled as she looked appreciatively at Molly's naked body, her slim waist, her large breasts swinging lightly with her movements, and the sweeping curve of her back down to her bare buttocks.

"Goodness, but you're a beauty," Mrs. Boatwright said. "Your skin is so creamy. I can't imagine how you've managed to stay single."

"Never met the right man, I guess," Molly said. The remark made her think unexpectedly of Charley Castle, and her eyes brimmed with tears.

"Well, if I was built like you," Mrs. Boatwright said, "I'd be busy."

Molly smiled through her tears as she tied the robe at her waist. She enjoyed her landlady's racy sense of humor, perhaps all the more so because Mrs. Boatwright herself was as strait-laced as a new corset.

She was an angular, heavy-featured woman in her mid-fifties, widowed for more than a decade. Her husband was thought to have been a wealthy man in Denver and had built a marble and brick mansion in the Capitol Hill district. But upon his sudden death, his widow discovered the Boatwright fortune to be the Boatwright debt.

To pay his creditors, Mrs. Boatwright convinced her husband's banker to let her keep the mansion. She would turn it into an exclusive boarding house for ladies of means only, and the income over a period of years would far outstrip the mortgage value. The plan not only worked, but after paying all the debts, Mrs. Boatwright prospered.

"Are you all right, Molly?"

Molly wiped a hand across her eyes. "It's this bathroom," she said. "Too steamy."

Two days later, on a sunny morning, a telegraphed message from New York City arrived for her. Molly received it at the front door of the boarding house and walked into the adjoining drawing room where she sat on a sofa covered with a silk and velvet quilt.

Taking the sheet of paper out of the envelope, she unfolded it and read the message.

Operative Molly Owens:

By now I presume you have received the Fenton file containing photographs and background information concerning our client, Winfield Shaw, and his current dilemma.

While I respect your strong sense of loyalty to the late Charles Castle, I regard your arrest in Denver to be an unfortunate incident. In all candor, I must suggest that your loyalty to the man was misplaced. He was a certifiable scoundrel, with a lengthy police record as a bunco artist.

Well documented, also, is your sterling record as a Fenton operative. You have brought many difficult cases, and a few that appeared to be impossible, to successful conclusions.

Your arrest was not connected with your work for the agency, and a court trial that could have put the Fenton Agency in bad light did not result. Therefore, I suggest that the incident is best forgotten.

Your investigative skills are needed by Mr. Shaw, and I trust you will accept this new assignment and go to work on it without delay. The New York papers have carried news of the immense gold discovery and the wild character of the Cripple Creek mining camp. I can say with confidence that this assignment will have its dangers, and your training in self-defense techniques and the use of weapons will be tested. If you require assistance, notify me by telegraph and I shall dispatch an operative to come to your aid as quickly as possible.

Horace J. Fenton
Fenton Investigative Agency
New York City, New York

Molly leaned back on the sofa. She had already read through the Shaw file, and examined his photographic portrait and the photographs of Cripple Creek and the famous Gold Hill nearby where Shaw had made his initial discovery that was now known as the Independence Mine.

An investigation had a beginning and an end. The satisfaction of searching out answers to questions, and the danger, gave her life a heightened sense of purpose. Molly needed that now more than ever.

CHAPTER III

The fast-paced boxing match within the square roped off in the middle of Myers Avenue looked to Molly more like a saloon brawl than a contest of fisticuffs under the rules of the Marquis of Queensberry.

Drawn here by the large crowd gathered in the street, Molly had walked down from the Cripple Creek railroad depot to watch the two bloodied miners batter one another with bare fists. Handbills advertised it as a grudge match between "Giant Powder George of the Independence Mine" and "Mule Kick Malloy of the Golden Opportunity Mine." Bets were placed, and the crowd of men and women urged the combatants on with loud shouts and cheers as fists landed on nose or jaw or slapped into bare midsection.

Cripple Creek sprawled out over a sloping hillside. Churches, schools, and the most elegant Victorian houses lined the narrow streets near the top of the hill, and the ramshackle row of saloons, gambling halls, and brothels were down here at the bottom on Myers Avenue.

Between these two extremes, as Molly had seen from the high ground of the railroad depot, was the crowded business district on Bennett Avenue.

Lined with dozens of stores, offices, banks, hotels, and restaurants, Bennett was an unusual main street. A section of it was on two levels where the hillside was steepest so that when wagon and horse traffic passed in opposite directions, one looked down on the other. Seeing this, Molly realized what a drummer on the train had meant when he'd said that a miner in Cripple Creek had gotten so drunk that he had fallen off the street. The two levels rejoined farther on toward the Palace Hotel and other frame and red brick establishments of town.

Surrounding Cripple Creek's orderly business and residential sections were countless shacks and cabins, and among them were the mines. Gold mines were everywhere, on every hillside and in every gulch. Half a mile away, Gold Hill swelled up out of the ground, a huge mound partially covered with aspen and pine trees.

Head frames like enormous gallows stood

over the mine shafts, some of which dropped hundreds of feet straight down into the earth, leading to underground networks of tunnels and more shafts. Around all the mines were heaps of rock and soil, oxidized to nearly every color of the rainbow. These were much more colorful than the rust-colored mine dumps Molly had seen west of Denver.

Far to the south of Cripple Creek, fifty miles distant, stood the long line of snowy peaks of the Sangre de Cristo Mountains, like lace turned up on the horizon. To the west, she saw the mountains of the Continental Divide, snowy, too. The rugged top of Pikes Peak was not far away, rising up from this mountain-top elevation of 9,494 feet above sea level.

To get there, Molly had ridden a southbound train from Denver to Colorado Springs, and there she had boarded a narrow-gauge line that cut west into the mountains. The trip was a beautiful one; the steam engine steadily pulled the passenger coaches and freight cars through rocky canyons with creeks churning through the bottoms, and meadows filled with colorful wildflowers and over mountains forested with pine and spruce and aspen trees.

As the train rounded a wide turn, the

shrill whistle of the steam engine sounded. Molly looked out through wavy glass in the passenger coach window and caught her first view of the richest gold field in the world.

Back in Denver, she had studied maps in the public library, and she had read newspaper accounts of Cripple Creek, but still she was not prepared for the dramatic sight of a booming city of 25,000 men, women, and children, most of whom had come here for no other reason than to make their fortunes.

"No criminals here," Molly had read in a Colorado Springs newspaper. "They've all gone to Cripple Creek."

Now as she stood at the edge of the crowd watching the fight, she looked at the men wearing slouch hats, overalls, and muddy boots. Obviously miners, they cheered the fighters in the ring. Other men wore trim black suits, starched collars and ties, and clean hats.

Molly guessed that most of the women in the crowd were saloon girls, some probably from the brothels and cribs farther down the street. Many of these women were loud and foul-mouthed, and when Mule Kick Malloy unexpectedly dropped Giant Powder George to the ground with a mighty blow to his abdomen, none of the men shouted curses louder than the women standing near Molly.

After brief arguments about Malloy's underhanded victory, bets were paid off. The people in the street began to mill about, and some drifted back to the saloons.

"Lucky!"

Overhearing a miner call out that name, Molly turned and saw a tall man wearing a black pinstriped suit and a bowler hat. She edged closer to him. From the Fenton file, she knew that a man named Leroy Luckett, owner of the Gold Coin Club, was known here as "Lucky."

Molly watched the miner joyfully collect a bet from Lucky, and then she discreetly moved into the tall man's line of vision. Taking on a worried expression, she pretended to be looking for something, glancing from one side of the street to the other. She soon caught his eye.

"May I be of service?" Lucky asked, moving closer to Molly.

She cast a brief smile at him but did not reply.

"I'm Leroy Luckett," he said, taking off his hat. A well-groomed man with a self-assured air about him, Luckett was square faced with dark eyes and a thin, black moustache on his upper lip.

"I'm on the right street," Molly said, "but with this crowd, I can't find my way."

"Which building are you looking for?" he asked.

"The Old Homestead," Molly replied.

Luckett barely concealed his surprise. "The Old Homestead," he repeated. "You don't look like a —" His voice trailed off.

"A whore?" Molly suggested, looking at him steadily.

"Well, I didn't mean —"

Molly moved away from him. "I'll find it on my own."

"Wait," Luckett said, clapping his bowler hat on his head and falling in step beside her. "The Old Homestead is down this way, on the other side of the street. I'll escort you through this crowd of rowdies." He added, "With your permission."

Molly nodded once in reply.

"I didn't catch your name," he said, holding out his arm for her.

"I didn't throw it," Molly replied. She walked on a few paces as they made their way through the men and women on the boardwalk; then she glanced at Luckett and put her hand on his arm. "Call me Molly," she said.

Luckett smiled and cast sidelong glances

at Molly as they walked along the boardwalk, passing saloons, gambling dens, and dance halls. Most were unpainted frame buildings with signs in large letters across the false fronts — Last Dollar Saloon, Bucket of Blood, Ducey's Exchange, Crapper Jack's, Marie's Dance Hall, and the Bulls-eye Saloon.

"Here's my place," Luckett said, gesturing to a small frame structure with curtained windows.

Molly heard tinkling piano music coming through the open door of the Gold Coin Club. She recognized the tune of "Do You Like Tutti-Frutti?" and she looked inside as they paused at the doorway. Along with a few upholstered chairs, an elaborately carved bar and back bar dominated the room, and far to the rear were felt-covered gambling tables.

"Gentlemen only in my establishment," Luckett said with a smile at Molly. "However, I might make an exception in your case."

They walked on, and after a pair of ore wagons rumbled past, Luckett led the way across the street where more drinking and gaming houses stood crowded against one another.

In front of the saloons Molly noticed

shaggy men dressed in dirty clothes, many wearing boots held together with wire. Obviously penniless and probably hungry, they stared at everyone who passed by.

"Looking for handouts," Luckett said with some disgust when he saw Molly looking at these men, "or an old friend who might be suckered for a grubstake." When they walked farther on, he added, "Don't come down here alone after dark, Molly. Some of these men are desperate. Others are just mean."

"I'll remember that," Molly said.

Beyond the saloon district were the brothels, quiet at this time of day. Some were only wooden shacks surrounded by heaps of trash and rusting cans and bottles glistening in the sunlight, but others were tidy board and batten buildings with red chintz curtains over the windows and flower boxes beneath the sills.

Bearing such names as Old Faithful, The Library, Kittens' Den, Lottie's Upstairs, they were two-story structures with parlors downstairs and "guest rooms" upstairs. The only brick building on the row was the Old Homestead.

Molly was impressed by it. Surrounded by a black wrought-iron fence, the Old Homestead looked as substantial and as sedate as a bank. The windows were heavily curtained with maroon drapes. The yard was clean. A walk of red brick led from the front gate to the door, and pansies bloomed beside the porch.

Molly passed through the gate as Luckett opened it. "Thank you, Mr. Luckett," she said, smiling at him.

He raised a hand to the brim of his bowler. "My pleasure to walk with a lovely woman," he said. Glancing past her to the door of the Old Homestead, he added, "I predict we'll meet again — soon."

CHAPTER IV

Molly found Pearl Devine, madam of the Old Homestead, to be a large, smiling woman with rich auburn hair piled on top of her head. She wore a pale yellow silk gown, strings of pearls around her neck, pearl earrings, and pearl rings mounted in gold on the fingers of each hand.

"You wasted no time in meeting Lucky," Pearl said as she closed the door.

Outside, Molly had seen a drape move in the front window, and as she came up the walk, she noticed a peephole in the center of the oak door. From Luckett, she had learned that admittance here was gained by recommendation or $100 in the manicured hand of a well-dressed man.

After explaining how she "happened" to meet Luckett, Molly followed Pearl down the front hall past a luxuriously furnished parlor, an adjoining gambling room, and on to a private bedroom at the rear of the building. Pearl held the door open for Molly, then came in behind her.

The floor of this small room was covered by a Persian carpet; on the walls were paintings of nude women, and across the room from a brass bed was a settee and matching upholstered chairs on either side of a low walnut table.

Pearl motioned for Molly to sit on the settee, then sat in a chair. "Does Lucky think you've come to work for me?"

Molly smiled as she sat on the settee and crossed her legs. "Right now he doesn't know what to think."

"Few people keep Lucky guessing for long," Pearl warned. "He's smooth as oil and shrewd."

"I hope to complete my investigation before he figures out what I'm up to," Molly said.

Pearl studied Molly for a moment. "I've never met a woman in your line of work before."

"More women are employed by investigative agencies than you might guess," Molly said.

"Well, it makes sense," Pearl said with a smile. "If you want to find out something, ask a woman."

"Tell me about the woman who lodged

the paternity suit against Mr. Shaw," Molly said. "I've been advised that she works for Leroy Luckett."

"That's right," Pearl said. "She lives in one of Lucky's cribs down the street. Goes by the name of Candace Smith. No telling what her real name is."

"And is she pregnant?" Molly asked.

Pearl nodded. "But not by Win Shaw. This lawsuit business is just a scheme for money." She added, "Of all the ways to get money from Win, this is the newest."

"What do you mean?" Molly asked.

"Oh, everyone on this blessed planet is after him for money," Pearl said disgustedly. "He gives it away by the bushel basket, but that isn't enough. People hound him wherever he goes, telling hard-luck stories that would make the devil himself shed a tear. You know, if Candace had told Win she was desperate for money, he'd have probably given her a handful. But not the $100,000 she's asking."

"What's her story?" Molly asked.

"She claims Win promised to marry her," Pearl said, "and backed out. She's a four-bit whore who's never seen anything better than a shack on Myers Avenue, much less the inside of Win's cabin."

"Cabin?" Molly asked in surprise.

"Win stays in his old prospecting cabin on Gold Hill when he's in Cripple Creek," Pearl said. "Sometimes I send a girl up to him. He doesn't come to town much anymore. Folks won't leave him alone down here."

Pearl smoothed the gown over her large thighs and went on. "In Colorado Springs, Win has a mansion for a winter home. He says he's happier up here in his cabin, though. He could buy every blueblood in the Springs, but he'll never be one of them. He's too good a man to stick his nose up in the air."

Hearing a note of pride in Pearl's voice, Molly said, "I look forward to meeting Mr. Shaw."

"He knew you were due in today," Pearl said, "and he told me to give you anything you need. You'll be hearing from him before long." She paused and added in a lower tone of voice, "Win and I are the only ones who know who you are and why you're here."

"Thanks for keeping the secret," Molly said.

"I wouldn't be in business without secrets," Pearl said with a smile. "You'd be surprised who some of my back-door clients are."

"Now I'm interested," Molly said.

Pearl chuckled. She glanced around the room. "This room is yours for as long as you need it. I'll give you a key so you can use the back door to come and go as you please. Did you bring any luggage?"

"I left it at the depot," Molly said.

Pearl nodded and stood. "I'll send for it right away so you can change out of your traveling clothes." As she moved to the door, she said over her shoulder, "My girls will be down for supper at five. You're welcome to join us."

"Thank you," Molly said, standing. "I will."

Pearl opened the door and stepped through it, then leaned back into the room. "Molly, be careful. There's a rough element around here, and they play for keeps."

After she was gone Molly looked around the room, poked her head into the curtained closet, then decided to use the water in the porcelain basin on the washstand. She undressed and unbuckled the holstered derringer strapped to the calf of her right leg.

After a sponge bath, she put on a silk robe from the closet, then sat on the settee and opened her handbag. Besides personal items, the tools of her work were inside.

Half a dozen magnifying lenses were encased in a leather pouch as well as skeleton keys on a ring and a set of locksmith's probes. Her revolver was in the handbag, too, a Colt Lightning Model .38, with a 2½-inch barrel, white bone grips, and scroll work on the nickel-plated frame.

Molly pulled the folded papers of the Fenton file out of the handbag. Among them was a photograph of Winfield Shaw. The forty-six-year-old bachelor was white haired and appeared gaunt with his drawn cheeks and sunken eyes. Molly wondered if the millionaire was as dour as he appeared.

Between the information here and Molly's own research, she knew a great deal about Shaw. Before his discovery of the Cripple Creek gold deposit, he was a Colorado Springs carpenter and cabinetmaker. Every weekend and spare moment for nearly twenty years, Shaw had prospected. He ranged far and wide through the Colorado Rockies without finding more than traces of gold, wearing out so many pairs of boots that his closest acquaintance became his cobbler. Shaw was known to carry on monologues with the donkeys that carried his prospecting gear. In Colorado Springs, the man was said to be "touched."

But he was not alone. Other men were

possessed by gold fever and used all their spare time and money to trudge over mountains and into remote canyons in search of a bonanza. Fortunes had been made that way.

On the Fourth of July 1891, Shaw made his first promising discovery practically in his back yard. Not even on a prospecting trip, he visited a cowboy friend on a high mountain ranch. Shaw came across an outcropping of sylvanite. Sylvanite meant gold to his practiced eye.

This deposit where Shaw later filed a claim became the Independence Mine and a year later was known to be the richest deposit ever found in the world. And others were nearby. In the space of twelve months, Winfield Shaw went from a $3.50-a-day carpenter to a $3,000-a-day mine owner.

Molly put the file away and stretched out on the bed. She closed her eyes. Thoughts of Charley Castle had drifted into her mind, and she wondered why.

Pursuit of a dream, she thought, was something Winfield Shaw and Charley Castle had in common. Molly knew that Charley had always believed he would strike it rich someday, somehow. Winfield Shaw must have nurtured such dreams, too, and Molly wondered if the millionaire

46

was anything like Charley.

After supper that night, she had a chance to find out. At nightfall, a top buggy arrived at the back door of the Old Homestead. Winfield Shaw had sent for Molly.

CHAPTER V

Winfield Shaw's cabin was on the side of Gold Hill that overlooked Cripple Creek. Molly first saw it by starlight when the buggy came up the narrow road far above the town and passed through a stand of aspen trees. Built of pine logs, the cabin had only two small windows on either side of the door and a sagging roof.

Molly climbed out of the buggy before the driver could come around and help her. She walked to the plank door of the cabin and knocked.

Moments later the door opened, and there stood Winfield Shaw. Like his photograph, he was gaunt and white haired, a man who looked closer to seventy than fifty. He wore a plain black suit with no crease in the trousers and a white shirt with a string tie.

"I'm Molly Owens," she said.

Shaw nodded and stepped back, motioning for her to enter.

The interior of the cabin amazed Molly and as she stepped inside, she understood Pearl's reference to her belief that Candace Smith, "a four-bit whore," had never set foot in this place.

The cabin was furnished like a palace in miniature. Molly came into the room, feeling her feet sink into a thick Brussels carpet. She stared at the carved furniture, obviously antique pieces from Europe: a teakwood table with a silver tea service on it, lamps of cut crystal, a chandelier hanging from the low ceiling, and gilt-framed oil paintings on the walls.

"My little joke on high society," Winfield Shaw said, closing the cabin door.

Molly was too amazed to speak for a long moment. Even the log walls had been paneled and covered with hand-painted wallpaper.

Shaw crossed the room to the table. "A cup of tea?" he asked. "Or coffee?"

"Tea," Molly said absently. Then she moved to the table and sat in the chair Shaw pulled out for her. She noticed that his hands were delicate as he poured tea into two cups, his wrists small, and his suit, while tailored, might as well have covered a skeleton.

Shaw offered a slice of lemon to Molly,

then sat across from her. "When your employer advised me that he was sending a woman operative, I didn't much like the idea. You're working in a man's world."

She met his steady gaze with a smile. "There's more to this world than men, Mr. Shaw."

A smile crept into the millionaire's expression. "Yeah, even a bachelor knows that." He drank, then set the cup down and conceded, "Your employer gave you the highest recommendation when I told him I wanted the best operative for this job. If I don't put a stop to this sort of thing, I'll spend the rest of my life in court denying fatherhood." He paused and added, "But frankly I'm not convinced a pretty lady like you can get the job done."

"I can't give you a guarantee, Mr. Shaw," Molly said. "The question is, now that you've seen me, do you want me to work for you, or don't you?"

Shaw's eyes widened, as he was obviously surprised by her candor. After studying her a moment, he said, "Yes, I do, Miss Owens. I do, at that."

"You can start by telling me everything you know about Candace Smith," Molly said. "I don't have any background information on her."

"That's because I don't know anything about her," Shaw said, his expression darkening. "Never even seen her, so far as I know."

"But you're acquainted with the man she works for," Molly said, "Leroy Luckett."

Shaw nodded. "As I wrote to Horace Fenton, we've had some dealings over the years. Lucky operated a saloon down in the Springs when I was driving nails and sawing wood for a living. About a year and a half ago, Lucky came to me and practically begged me to buy a claim he'd won in a poker game. Really, I think he was mad because some prospector had unloaded on him the most unpromising piece of ground you ever saw. I bought it for a high price because it adjoins another claim of mine."

"Did you work Lucky's claim?" Molly asked.

"Yeah," Shaw said, "I sank that shaft two-hundred feet before I struck good sylvanite. For six months, it was one of the better producers on Gold Hill."

"What was Lucky's reaction to the strike?" Molly asked.

Shaw shrugged. "I heard he was mad about the whole thing, but I don't know why he should be. The money I spent sinking that shaft two-hundred feet without

51

a dime in return was more cash than Lucky has seen in his life. Even my mine foreman was beginning to think I was loco."

"Do you think Lucky is behind this lawsuit?" Molly asked.

"He might be," Shaw said, "but I doubt it. The young lady wants to retire on my money. This scheme is probably as simple as that. I want you to trip her up."

Molly nodded. For some reason, she found herself thinking of Charley Castle. The man believed in his own destiny, believed he was marked for greatness. Molly wondered if Shaw held the same belief.

She asked, "Did you know you'd strike it rich on Lucky's claim?"

"I had a hunch," Shaw said slowly, "but some of my hunches have been wrong. You see, this whole mining district is an ancient volcano, a huge one. The mountains around here are what's left of the rim."

He leaned forward and made a cup of his hands. "Down in the bottom, gold ore became molten and ran into fissures in the rock. That's why the ore is so pure when we strike a vein underground. I happened to hit one on the claim I bought from Lucky."

Shaw paused, smiling faintly. "But I reckon you didn't come here to talk mining."

"I'm interested," Molly said. "Maybe I'll catch gold fever myself."

"You'll have a happier life if you don't," he replied. "Most people who seek gold keep themselves poor, and a few make too damned much money to ever be happy again."

Molly heard a tone of philosophical sadness in his voice and watched him stare at the polished wood grain in the table top. After a long silence he looked up and cast an ironic smile at her.

"But we can't change our circumstances," he said.

"No, I suppose not," Molly said. She stood and shook hands with him. "In the next few days, I'll let you know if I've made progress in my investigation."

Shaw nodded. He came around the table and crossed the room with her to the door. "If you need anything, Miss Owens, tell Pearl. She can get a message to me, day or night."

Riding down the hillside in the buggy, Molly thought back on the evening. She saw a certain similarity of temperament between Winfield Shaw and Charley Castle. Both men were reflective by nature. And both saw themselves as outsiders, often looking at life as theater with characters playing out various roles. They themselves did not fit into the play.

The buggy reached the slum outskirts of Cripple Creek. Molly realized that she had to stop thinking about Charley. He was dead, gone from her life forever, and she must stop trying to find him in other men.

Entering the Old Homestead through the back door, she heard piano music in the front parlor; then came a burst of laughter. In a private room next to the parlor were gambling tables and a bar. Molly had been given a brief tour after eating supper with "the girls." She had been impressed by the luxurious quality of the furnishings and by the number of people who earned a living there. Besides the eight girls who lived upstairs, Pearl employed a cook, a maid, two bartenders, and the piano player.

No gamblers worked in the Old Homestead. Pearl explained that she had learned by hard experience that men often blamed their losses on professional gamblers. To avoid fights, she developed a policy of allowing her clients and the girls to operate the roulette wheel or the faro table themselves. The gambling then became good-natured, leaving the losers no one to blame but the fates.

Molly entered her room, and had been

there only a few minutes when she heard a tapping on the door. She opened it to find Pearl in the hallway, smelling of perfume and cigar smoke.

"Lucky came in about an hour ago," she said, "and asked for you. I told him you were indisposed."

Molly smiled. Indisposed. She liked that word. It covered many possibilities, none serious and none of which could be argued by a client in the Old Homestead.

"Is he still here?" Molly asked.

Pearl nodded. "He's in the gambling room."

"I'll see him," Molly said.

Molly followed Pearl into the plush gambling parlor, a smoky room lighted by gas lamps. A dozen or more men crowded around the roulette wheel with several of Pearl's girls.

Other men stood at the bar, leaning back on their elbows, each man with a polished boot propped against the brass foot rail. One left the bar. He was tall, his black hair gleamed in the dim light, and he came across the room in long strides, smiling.

Molly forced herself to smile as she greeted Leroy Luckett.

CHAPTER VI

"My prediction comes true," Luckett said, striding across the carpeted floor of the gambling parlor. He smiled broadly at Molly. "We meet again."

"All according to your plan, Mr. Luckett," Molly said.

"Well, yes," he said, glancing at Pearl. "I did ask for you, and now I'm honored by your lovely presence."

"Watch him," Pearl said. "Lucky can lay it on thick." She moved away, walking toward the sliding door that separated this room from the front parlor.

"Champagne?" Luckett asked, undaunted by Pearl's remark. He motioned to the bar where the other men casually regarded them. "We can take our goblets of sparkling wine to your room for more private conversation."

Molly shook her head and saw his practiced smile fade. He was dressed in a broadcloth suit with a starched white shirt and tie, and his black hair shone with oil. He carried with him odors of bay-rum tonic and sweat.

"Well, then," Luckett said, smiling again, "we can take our wine in the front parlor."

At that moment, a shriek went up from the girls standing with the men at the roulette wheel. A buxom, redheaded woman, appropriately named Red Rose, had won a large sum of money for the portly, gray-haired man at her side. Hands clutching greenbacks and gold and silver coins, Red Rose hugged him and planted a kiss on his gleaming forehead, leaving a smear of rouge behind.

Molly said to Luckett, "Yes, I'd like that."

"Then everyone is lucky tonight," he said, nodding at the men and women gathered around the roulette wheel. He went to the bar and handed three twenty-dollar gold pieces to the bartender, then came back and took Molly's arm.

He led her into the front parlor. The gas lights were turned low, and the couples seated on sofas were shadowy figures. At the far end of the room, the pianist softly played the melody of "Jeanie with the Light Brown Hair."

Molly sat with Luckett on an unoccupied

sofa and felt him move so close that his thigh pressed against hers. He took her hand and wetly kissed it, then leaned closer and whispered:

> I dream of Jeanie with the light
>   brown hair,
> Borne, like a vapor, on the summer
>   air;
> I see her tripping where the bright
>   streams play,
> Happy as the daisies that dance on
>   her way.

He brought his hand up and stroked her cheek, whispering, "Jeanie could not have been lovelier than you."

The bartender entered the parlor. On a silver tray, he carried a bottle of French champagne and two cut-glass goblets. Bowing, he set the bottle and goblets on the low table in front of Molly and Luckett, poured bubbling champagne, and departed.

Luckett whispered a toast to Molly's "eternal beauty," and moved his other hand along the top of her thigh. Molly felt a surge of anger.

"You're going farther than conversation, Mr. Luckett," she said, grasping his wrist. She saw his teeth gleam in the semidarkness as he smiled and pushed his hand farther up her thigh.

Using a jujitsu principle, Molly suddenly pulled his wrist toward her. The moment he involuntarily resisted, she pushed his wrist away, very hard.

Luckett's arm snapped away. He swore in surprise, spilling wine from the goblet he held.

Molly drained the champagne from her goblet in one swallow, feeling a mild jolt followed by a tingling sensation in her nostrils. She was repulsed by Luckett, yet at the same time she hoped the dim light concealed her expression. She thrust her goblet out to him for a refill and tried to smile.

Still surprised and growing angry, Luckett scowled at her. Then he picked up the bottle and filled Molly's glass. He emptied his, gulped it down, and refilled it.

Molly watched as he drew a cigar from his coat pocket, trimmed the end, and fired it. The match flame danced in his dark eyes while he puffed, and then he blew it out with a breath of fragrant smoke.

Luckett regarded Molly while he smoked. He emptied his goblet of champagne again before breaking the long silence. "I'm in the habit of getting what I want. And I want you." He added, "Pearl said you were indisposed tonight. I'll let it go at that — this time."

Molly tried to smile as though all was forgiven. "Tell me about yourself, Mr. Luckett. I've heard you're an important man in Cripple Creek and Colorado Springs."

"I own some properties," he said. After another goblet of champagne, his tongue loosened, and Luckett spoke vaguely of owning several mines in the Cripple Creek district, hinting at great wealth.

Molly said, "I suppose you're nearly as wealthy as the famous Winfield Shaw, aren't you?"

Luckett's expression darkened at the mention of Shaw's name, and he became silent.

"Winfield Shaw is constantly written up in the Denver newspapers," Molly said. "I've heard he's one of the wealthiest men in the country now."

Luckett grunted and in the next quarter of an hour said little while he downed the champagne. Belching, he stood, bid Molly good night in a slurred voice, and lurched out.

After he was gone, Pearl came to the sofa and sat beside Molly. "Find out anything?"

Molly shook her head.

"What do you plan to do next?" Pearl asked.

"Meet Candace Smith," Molly said.

The sky over Cripple Creek was pure blue and very bright when Molly stepped out the door of the Old Homestead the next morning. Breathing the crisp, cool air, she followed the boardwalk along Myers Avenue, walking away from the saloon district. At the end of the block, she saw the cribs lining the street ahead.

Built of an odd assortment of boards and logs, of discarded doors and window frames, the cribs were no more than shabby bedrooms lining the street, one after another, inches apart. All were unpainted, and most were unnamed. The boards and logs were weathered to a gray-brown color, warped and cracked, stained at every haphazard joint by rusting nails.

No boardwalks were on this ramshackle block that marked the end of Myers Avenue. Molly picked her way through wagon-wheel ruts and stepped around horse droppings as she walked in front of the cribs. At this hour, all was quiet, and the street was empty. In the distance, back toward the depot, Molly heard the shrill whistle of a steam engine, and from the next block came a tumble of heavy ore wagons and shouts of teamsters.

In the middle of the block, on the left side of the street, Molly found the crib Pearl had described to her. A round, stained-glass window graced the door of the weathered shack, and from the angle of the tarpaper roof protruded a length of black stovepipe.

Molly rapped on the door. She waited, and hearing no response, knocked again. A groggy voice came from within, and several moments later the door opened.

The woman who moved into the doorway wore a tattered robe and was barefoot. She was pale, gray-eyed, and her dark hair, unwashed, clung to her head like a cap.

"What . . . you want?" she asked in a slurred voice.

"Candace Smith?" Molly asked.

"Yeah."

"I'm Molly Owens," Molly said. "We have a mutual friend in Denver, Sarah Perkins, and she suggested I call on you while I'm visiting in town."

Blinking slowly, Candace stared blankly at Molly. "Never heard of her."

"Well, Sarah certainly knows you," Molly said, smiling. "And she told me that if there was anything you needed, I should give it to you. Sarah feels a debt of gratitude to you."

Candace eyed her. "She does, eh."

"That's right," Molly said. "On Market Street in Denver, you were practically next-door neighbors."

"I worked on Market — while back."

Molly smiled. "That's what Sarah told me." She glanced past the woman. "Mind if I come in?"

Candace half turned and stopped. "The place is a mess —"

"Oh, that's all right," Molly said cheerfully. She edged past the woman and entered the crib.

CHAPTER VII

An iron bed with sagging springs, a small parlor stove beside a washstand of rough pine, and a wicker rocking chair and clothing trunk were the only furnishings in the crib. There was hardly room for anything else.

When Candace closed the door, Molly turned and saw colorful bands of sunlight streaming through the stained-glass window, spilling colors across the bed like a broken rainbow. On the washstand, Molly had noticed a vial of laudanum and now understood why the woman's speech was slurred and why she was groggy.

"I'm visiting Pearl down at the Old Homestead," Molly said. "She told me that you're pregnant."

Candace nodded, still eying Molly with suspicion.

"We'll take up a collection in the Old Homestead," Molly went on, "and I know Sarah will contribute."

Candace shrugged indifferently. "Every pregnant whore gets money. Then what?"

"What are your plans, Candace?" Molly asked.

She looked at Molly as though the question had no meaning. Moving to the wicker rocking chair, Candace grasped the arms and lowered herself into it. She motioned for Molly to sit on the bed.

"My back's been hurting for a month," Candace said. "Spend most of my time in this chair."

Bedsprings creaked as Molly sat on the rumpled wool blanket that covered the mattress.

"I never went by the name of Candace up in Denver," she said, casting a challenging look at Molly.

Molly smiled, wondering how much longer she could keep this fictional Sarah Perkins alive. Pearl had mentioned that she'd heard Candace had been in Denver at one time, and Molly had guessed right that the woman had worked in Denver's Tenderloin District.

"You were Maria, weren't you?" Molly asked. "Or Maryanne?"

Candace's eyes narrowed as though she herself could not remember. "Ellie," she said at last. "Ellie."

"Oh, yes," Molly said. "Sarah heard about you from one of her clients who had been down here in Cripple Creek."

"Ellie," Candace said a third time. "I was young then." She paused. "Nobody wants me now, pregnant or not. Too old." She closed her eyes.

Molly saw tears roll down her cheeks. Leaving the bed, Molly knelt in front of her and took her hand.

"I want to help you, Candace."

The woman's eyes did not open. She slowly rocked back and forth, crying silently. After a time, she began rambling about a lover of long ago who'd promised to marry her. He had gone away somewhere and never returned.

Candace opened her eyes and held out her right hand. On the ring finger was a gold ring with a small, twinkling diamond.

"I'll never sell this," Candace said hoarsely. "Never . . . no matter how hungry —"

She was clinging to the only hope left to her, Molly realized, this lost lover who had given her a diamond ring. "Would you like to leave Cripple Creek?"

"Leave," Candace replied as though the idea was impossible.

"You can go to Denver and stay at my

place," Molly said. "I have a room in a beautiful mansion on Capitol Hill."

For a moment, Candace's expression brightened, then faded. "I can't . . . leave here."

"Why?" Molly asked.

Candace did not answer. She closed her eyes and leaned back.

"It's because of a man, isn't it?" Molly asked. "You're afraid of a certain man."

After a long silence, Candace whispered, "You know how this business is."

"I know it doesn't have to be that way," Molly said.

"Maybe not for you," Candace said, opening her eyes. "You're young."

"You don't have to live in fear," Molly said.

"I reckon you don't understand, after all," Candace said.

"Then tell me," Molly said, "so I will understand."

Candace made no reply.

"His name is Leroy Luckett, isn't it?" Molly asked.

Eyes widening in surprise, Candace slowly leaned forward in the rocker. "Who are you? What the hell . . . you want?"

"I want to help you," Molly said again, realizing that even though the woman's mind was dulled by laudanum, she now doubted

Molly's story. "I want to help get you out of this mess with Winfield Shaw."

Candace sank back into the rocker, eying Molly. "You'd better get out of here."

"Luckett put you up to this paternity suit, didn't he?" Molly asked. "Mr. Shaw is not the father of your child."

Candace made no reply, but fear had widened her eyes.

Molly squeezed her hand. "Candace, you're being used."

"I've been used by men all my life," she said.

"But this is your chance to stop it," Molly said. "What's Luckett offering you — money? He'll never get a dime from Shaw."

Candace exhaled tiredly. "Oh, hell," she whispered.

"You can trust me," Molly said.

"I never thought this damned scheme of Lucky's would work," she said quietly. "Shaw will get a bunch of lawyers —"

"I have a place for you to go," Molly said, "and I'll give you enough money for a new start."

"What do you mean — exactly?" she asked.

"You can stay with me in Denver," Molly said, "until you find a place to live. I'll make sure you get enough money for all your expenses. You can have your baby, buy new clothes, and get a new start."

Her expression clouded with doubt. "I don't even know you . . . didn't catch your name." She added, "And I never heard of Sarah-what's-her-name up in Denver."

"But you can trust me," Molly said again. Releasing the woman's hand, she opened her handbag and took out fifty dollars. She folded the bills into Candace's limp hand.

"There's some expense money," Molly said. "I'll buy two train tickets to Denver, and we'll leave on the next train."

Now Candace stared at her, a mixture of hope and fear on her face.

"Candace," Molly said, "if you leave Cripple Creek now, you'll leave this crib behind. You'll start a new life with your child, a life without fear of any man."

Candace sobbed. Tears rolled down her cheeks, and she covered her face with her hands.

Molly knew she had to work fast. Candace might return to her opium drug and forget everything — or convince herself it had all been a dream. Worse, Luckett might get to her before Molly could return and talk or coerce the woman into changing her mind.

Molly hurried back to the Old Homestead, undressed, and put on her riding clothes and boots. Leaving through the back door, she crossed the street to the next block where she'd seen a livery stable. After renting a saddle horse, she rode out of Cripple Creek at a high lope and followed the ore-wagon road that wound up the side of Gold Hill.

Shaw was not in his cabin. A guard armed with a shotgun was there, the same man who had driven Molly in the buggy to meet Shaw, and he directed her to the Independence Mine farther down the road.

Half a mile away, Molly found the big mine on a sloping meadow ringed by pine trees. From earlier research, she'd learned that this had been pasture land before Shaw made his discovery. A lone rancher years before had driven cattle across a nearby creek, and several were lamed while picking their way on the rocky bottom. "Cripple Creek," the ranchman had angrily called it, and the name stuck.

A gallowslike head frame towered over the shaft of the Independence Mine. Thick cables ran from a set of pulleys at the top straight down into the gaping hole of the shaft. The cables pulled loaded ore buckets up and lowered empty ones into the depths where, by candlelight, men worked the gold veins with hand drills and sledgehammers. When a shift ended, the same cables sent a steel cage down and brought miners to the surface, then lowered a new crew to the tunnels hundreds of feet below.

The whole operation was powered by a huffing steam engine housed in a shack near the base of the head frame. As Molly rode toward it and the other mine buildings, she saw a group of men at the shaft where the steel cage was suspended. They wore overalls stained with black grease and splattered with mud. Molly was a dozen yards away before she realized one of them was Winfield Shaw. She reined up and dismounted.

Two mechanics were inside the steel cage, working on a pulley at the top of it. One of the men turned a large crank, and the cage raised a few inches. Turning the crank the opposite way, the cage lowered.

"Okay, try it now!" Shaw called to a man operating the steam engine. As he turned, he saw Molly. His eyes widened in surprise.

Shaw stayed there long enough to see that the pulley in the cage worked properly under steam power; then he left the men and came toward Molly, a questioning look on his dour face.

CHAPTER VIII

"Ten thousand dollars!" Winfield Shaw exclaimed. "This is blackmail!"

"No, it isn't," Molly replied. "It's philanthropy."

They had moved away from the huffing steam engine in the shack and walked past a pile of coal until they were out of earshot of the men working there and around the head frame. Molly held the reins of the saddle horse while she talked to Shaw.

"I'm paying you to award ten thousand dollars to a whore I've never laid eyes on?" he demanded. "This is a joke — and I'm on the butt end of it."

"Mr. Shaw," Molly said, "Candace is not your enemy in this matter. She's a victim who's being used. Leroy Luckett put her up to this paternity suit."

"Are you certain of that?" Shaw asked in a low voice.

Molly related her conversation with

Candace. "She was loaded with laudanum, and I got more out of her than I might have otherwise. I believe her. She has no reason to lie. What she wants most is to get out of this mess. But she can't see a way, and she's afraid. She's afraid of having this baby, and she's afraid of Luckett."

"Luckett," Shaw growled, the truth still sinking in.

"If Candace leaves town," Molly said, "his scheme is finished."

Shaw reluctantly conceded the point.

"And the money will give her a new start in life."

"A lot of people believe money has that magical power," Shaw said. He paused. "Well, how much cash do you need?"

"Five hundred dollars," Molly said. "I'll buy Candace a train ticket and give the rest of the cash to her. I'll take her to Denver myself."

"All right," Shaw said, nodding. He thought a moment, then added, "I'll have my lawyer draw up a document for her to sign. The woman will have to admit in writing that she lied. After she does and after she's out of Cripple Creek for good, I'll send her the ten thousand. Not that money ever brings happiness to anyone."

"This money will keep her alive," Molly said, "and it'll buy time for her. That's what she needs."

Shaw shook his head, clearly believing that he was in possession of a larger truth.

Molly did not argue the point, but she saw deep irony in the fact that Winfield Shaw had spent much of his life seeking a bonanza, and now that he had it, he continually disavowed it. But at the same time, the man never offered to give his millions away and live a life of joyous poverty.

Shaw returned to the shack housing the steam engine and presently came back with a note scrawled in pencil.

"Give this to Clint Lange," he said, handing the note to her. "He's in my office on the second floor of the Cripple Creek Bank on Bennett."

Molly folded the note in half and slipped it into the pocket of her riding skirt. She mounted the saddle horse and turned the animal.

"Now I know what Mr. Fenton meant," Shaw said, "when he told me he was sending his best operative. You've done a good job — quickly."

Molly saw a brief smile cross his dour face, and she returned it as she touched her heels to the horse and rode away.

The Cripple Creek Bank was a handsome

two-story brick building on the corner of Bennett and Third, in the heart of the bustling town. Molly had not taken time to return the horse to the livery and change clothes, and she was aware of some stares as she tied the saddle horse at the post in front of the bank and went inside. Proper ladies wore long, dark dresses, and Molly knew that she would be considered eccentric by those who saw her that morning.

Crossing the lobby to a wide staircase, she climbed to the second floor. Upon reaching the landing, she saw that offices lined the hallway, and then to her right she heard men's voices raised in argument.

Drawn there, Molly walked past the closed doors of the offices, reading the names painted in gold letters on each one. An open transom over the last door was where the shouts came from. The sign on the door read: *Shaw Enterprises, Clinton Lange.*

A moment after Molly read it, the door was flung open.

"Out of here before I pick you up and throw you out!" yelled a large, square-shouldered man with flowing brown hair combed back from his forehead.

The object of his anger was a slender, balding man wearing thick spectacles. He was dressed in work clothes that were pressed and appeared to be little used.

Molly watched as he met the larger man's angry stare long enough to prove he was unafraid, then turned to the open door. His eyebrows shot up in surprise when he saw Molly. Hesitating a moment, he moved past her and strode down the hallway.

"I'm looking for Mr. Lange," Molly said when the bespectacled man was gone.

"Well, you found him," he said through a clenched jaw. But as he cast a second look at Molly, his expression softened, and he stepped to one side. "Come in."

Although Clint Lange wore a tie and starched collar, a tailored suit and gleaming black shoes, he looked like he belonged outdoors. His complexion was ruddy, and his hands were large.

Strangely, Molly thought as she entered the plush office, the man who had just been invited to leave looked more like he belonged in here than Clint. And Clint was a man who might have been more comfortable in work clothes of heavy cotton and a pair of hobnailed boots on his feet.

The office was carpeted and furnished with maple chairs and a large maple desk cluttered with papers. On the walls, above the wainscoting, were paintings of Rocky Mountain peaks, meadows populated with deer and elk, and Molly saw one large oil on canvas that depicted the Independence Mine.

Clint pulled a chair to the front of the desk. After Molly was seated in it, he rounded the desk in a few swift steps and sat in his black-leather swivel chair.

"How can I help you, Miss — ?"

"Owens," Molly said. "I'm Molly Owens. I work for Mr. Shaw."

"Oh?" Clint asked, vaguely surprised.

Molly took the note from her pocket, unfolded it, and handed it across the desk to him. For an instant, her fingers touched his warm hand, and she was unexpectedly stirred.

Clint nodded as he read the scrawled note on the paper. Evidently, he had seen such messages before. "All right, we'll go downstairs and I'll withdraw five hundred dollars for you." But he continued looking at Molly, making no move to get up.

Molly met his frank stare. He was a handsome man with a straightforward way about him and a penetrating manner.

"Just what is it you're doing for Win?" Clint asked at last. He added, "If I may ask."

"You may ask," Molly said, "but I may not answer."

Clint laughed suddenly. He started to get up from his chair, then stopped. "Wait, I think I know. Win told me he'd hired a Fenton operative, a woman. You're investigating that paternity suit, aren't you?"

Molly did not reply. She believed that Clint Lange was a trustworthy man, and Shaw probably confided in him. But she had not been told to confide in him, and for that reason she decided not to confirm his guess, accurate as it was.

"I swear, Win will do anything to get out from under that nuisance paternity suit," Clint said. "He has bigger problems that he should worry about more."

"Like that man you just pitched out of your office?" Molly asked.

Clint grinned. "You're not answering my question, so why should I answer yours?"

"Touché, Mr. Lange," Molly said.

"Call me Clint," he said, still grinning. He looked at her appraisingly, then said, "We have a common interest in what's best for Win. I'll answer your question."

He leaned back in the chair. "You may have heard talk about labor troubles brewing. Cripple Creek miners want more money, and there's a lot of union talk going around. That little weasel who was just in here, Riley Newcomb, is an organizer. He announced to me that things would go easy for the Independence if Win would raise wages half a dollar to set an example for the other mine owners in the district."

"Will he do it?" Molly asked.

"If he gives in to those outlaws," Clint said, "he'll do it over my dead body."

Molly left the Cripple Creek Bank with five hundred dollars stuffed into the pockets of her riding skirt. She mounted the saddle horse and rode up Bennett to the railroad depot, passing in the next block along the lower level of the divided street.

The depot, steep roofed and built of red brick, was surrounded by benches and wheeled carts used by porters when a train came in. Behind the depot stretched a long loading platform next to three sets of narrow-gauge rails.

Molly tied the horse at a hitching post and climbed the steps into the depot. Along the far wall, a clerk wearing a green visor sat in a cage. Head bowed, he was reading a copy of the *Police Gazette.*

The clerk pried his attention away from the vivid descriptions of murder and mayhem long enough to sell Molly two tickets to Denver on the next train, departing at one o'clock that afternoon.

Molly looked up at the clock on the wall. She had less than two hours.

Riding the horse down slope on Bennett, Molly turned at First Street and rode down to Myers. On the avenue ahead, she saw a crowd on one side of the street, and as a black hearse came from the opposite direction and drew up there, she realized the crowd was clustered around the door of Candace Smith's crib.

CHAPTER IX

Galloping down Myers to the next block, Molly reined the horse to a sliding halt at the edge of the crowd. She jumped out of the saddle and pushed her way through the knot of people but was abruptly stopped by a uniformed deputy standing in the open doorway of the crib.

"You can't go in there," he said, folding his arms over his chest.

Molly saw an impassive expression on his face. The lawman wore a dark blue uniform with brass buttons, and on his head was a cap with a short bill that gleamed in the sunlight.

Edging to one side, Molly looked past his shoulder and saw into the crib. Sprawled on the floor was the body of Candace Smith. Her face, pale in life, was now whitened by death. On her forehead was a red gash surrounded by a purple bruise.

"I'm a friend," Molly said. Ignored by the

deputy, she said in a louder voice, "I was here visiting with Candace earlier this morning."

"Let her in," came a deep, commanding voice inside the crib.

The big deputy half turned, and Molly stepped past him. Inside was another lawman in uniform with gold braid on his cap. Behind him stood two attendants from the hearse.

"What happened?" Molly asked.

"I'll ask the questions, miss. I'm Marshal Broyles. Who are you?"

"Molly Owens," she said, pulling her gaze away from the corpse to look at him. He was clean shaven, deep voiced, and his face resembled a bulldog's, with his loose jowls, blunt nose, and thick lips.

"What time of day were you in here?" Broyles asked.

"About nine-thirty this morning," Molly replied. Broyles motioned with the toe of his black boot to two empty vials of laudanum on the floor. "What was her condition at that hour?"

"She was awake," Molly said. While Broyles stared at her, Molly added, "We had a long conversation."

"About what?" he asked.

"Does it matter?" Molly asked. "Candace

82

was awake and talking to me, and she was all right when I left."

Broyles gave Molly an appraising look. "You don't live in Cripple Creek, do you, Miss Owens?"

"I'm from Denver," Molly said. "So was Candace."

Broyles nodded, coming to the conclusion Molly intended. "Does she have family up there? Anyone who'd claim her body?"

Molly shook her head.

"You live on a ranch out of Denver?" he asked.

Molly again became aware of her clothes. "No, I was out riding this morning." She looked at the town marshal. "Tell me what happened. Who killed her?"

"No one," he said with a shrug. "She was probably stumbling around here under the influence of laudanum, fell, and cracked her skull on the bedstead."

"But how was the body discovered?" she asked.

"The back door was ajar," Broyles said. "The girl in the next crib noticed it, came in, and found her."

Molly turned and looked out through the open door, seeing an outhouse and piles of trash and rusting cans on the ground. Turning back to Broyles, she asked, "How much money did you find in here?"

"A few coins in her coat pocket," Broyles said. "Why?"

"I gave her fifty dollars," Molly said.

"Well, the neighbor girl might have cleaned her out," he said. "Or maybe Candace spent it on laudanum. It's happened before, miss. The girls down on this end of the row ain't got much to live for."

The lawman's indifference suddenly angered Molly, and she glared at him.

Broyles met her stare, then asked, "If she was murdered, who do you think did it — Winfield Shaw?"

The two men who had brought the hearse laughed at the absurd suggestion.

"I don't know who did it," Molly said. "Finding the killer is a job for the police."

"Everybody's ready to tell us what to do," Broyles said tiredly. He moved to the front door of the crib. "My judgment is that this was an accidental death, and that's the way it'll be recorded." Over his shoulder, he said, "Take her away, boys." The marshal stepped outside and ordered the crowd to move back.

Molly watched the attendants unceremoniously carry the body out of the crib to the hearse outside. Pulled by matched black horses, the hearse soon rolled away, turning in the middle of the street to head back the way it had come. Marshal Broyles and his deputy left, and the crowd dispersed soon afterward.

Molly quickly searched the crib but found nothing out of the ordinary until she discovered tangled strands of hair on the floor. Picking up the large clump of hair, she examined the strands. The color was Candace's, and no magnifying lens was needed to see that the hairs had been pulled out by the roots.

Had Luckett been here? Molly wondered. Candace might have told him that she was leaving Cripple Creek, and during an argument Luckett might have clubbed her — or grabbed her by the hair, Molly suddenly realized, and bashed her head against the iron bedstead. If he'd left through the back door, he could have departed unseen from the street. And the empty laudanum vials were planted evidence that had led Marshal Broyles to an obvious conclusion.

Suspicion was one thing, proof was another. Molly had no proof, not a shred. All she had now was deep rage. This pregnant woman had been murdered and robbed. Molly was convinced of that and believed that if Candace were not a prostitute on the low end of Myers, the marshal would have looked into her death more closely.

Molly let go of the tangled hairs, watching them drift to the bare plank floor. Filled with sudden disgust, she crossed the room to the front door. It stood partly open. The stained-glass window in the door was the only cheery thing here, but at this time of day the leaded pieces of glass were muted.

Stepping outside, Molly saw her saddle horse standing in the empty street, patiently waiting with the reins trailing on the ground. She closed the door behind her and went to the horse. The animal lifted his head and looked at her, ears cocked.

Molly picked up the reins, and as she turned to mount, her eye was caught by movement in the window of the crib next door. Remembering what Marshal Broyles had said, Molly left the horse and went to the door of the crib.

She knocked and waited. No answer came, and she knocked again, harder. Several more minutes passed before the door slowly opened.

"I wasn't dressed." The small voice belonged to a fat woman with strawberry-blonde hair combed to the top of her head. She was round faced, with puffy cheeks and full lips.

"Candace Smith was a friend of mine," Molly said.

The woman looked downward, shaking her head sadly.

"Marshal Broyles told me that you found the body," Molly said. When the woman looked up, Molly asked, "Did you see anyone go into the crib or leave before you found her?"

"No," the woman whispered.

Molly asked, "Are you certain?" She added, "If you need money, I'll pay —"

"No," she said emphatically. "I didn't see anyone." She closed the door.

Molly stood there a moment, wondering if the woman was lying or if she simply wanted no part of this trouble.

Returning to the horse, Molly swung up into the saddle and rode down the street. An act of violence had brought this case to an abrupt halt. Her work was done, but she felt unsettled. A job was unfinished.

By all her instincts, Molly wanted to investigate the murder of Candace Smith. She had some leads to follow up. But she knew that after she reported to Winfield Shaw, she would no longer have a client in Cripple Creek.

CHAPTER X

Molly returned the saddle horse to the livery stable, paid her bill, and walked back to the Old Homestead. She found Pearl seated at the table in the dining room, giving the day's instructions to the cook. The midday meal here was served at two in the afternoon, with a light evening meal at five. Then Pearl's girls dressed and went to work when "guests" began arriving an hour or so later.

The cook was a young Irish girl named Colleen, "fresh off the boat," Molly had heard her described. She was slender and energetic, with lovely natural coloring in her face, now wearing a long cotton dress and full-length white apron.

Colleen listened intently to Pearl's orders; then with a "Yes, ma'am," she turned and bustled into the kitchen.

Molly sat at the dining-room table beside Pearl and told her what had happened that morning.

"No!" Pearl said, shocked. "Poor woman." She paused. "I didn't admire her for what she was trying to do to Win, but I can understand what drove her to it."

"Leroy Luckett drove her to it," Molly said. She went on to explain the facts she had learned that morning and what she now suspected.

Pearl reacted with strong disbelief. "Lucky's a schemer, and he may be enough of a scoundrel to put Candace up to that lawsuit. But I can't believe he'd murder the girl. I just can't."

Pearl thought a moment, then said, "You know, Molly, those four-bit cribs attract the worst men in town. The women there are all alone. Robbery and even murder are common on that end of Myers."

"Marshal Broyles has certainly learned to accept it as a fact of life," Molly said. She related some of her conversation with him.

"Broyles has always treated me fairly," Pearl said. "He knows this town inside out. He might be right about Candace's death, you know."

Molly saw the beginnings of a disagreement on this point. To avoid one, she conceded that was a possibility. But she kept her private thoughts to herself.

"Well," Molly said, changing the subject,

"now I have to report to Mr. Shaw."

"You look like you need to lie down," Pearl said with a sympathetic smile. "Leave it to me to get word to Win. He'll send a buggy."

At two in the afternoon, Molly sat at the dining-room table with Pearl's girls, eight young women who were beautiful even now with scrubbed faces, hair pinned up, and dressed in long housecoats and slippers. Molly sat between Red Rose and a raven-haired woman named Jane.

Colleen served the meal. The women's conversation was not about men but ran to pleasant talk of everyday matters: a new millinery in town, the best clothier in Colorado Springs, and a newfangled curling iron a drummer had sold to Jane the previous week.

Molly had been introduced to them only as a friend of Pearl's. If the women were curious about her presence, they did not reveal it. They were polite to her and asked no questions. Perhaps, in return, they wanted no questions asked.

Pearl ruled the Old Homestead with quiet, firm authority, and Molly had sensed almost immediately that no one crossed her. Probably no one wanted to. Pearl's girls were the highest paid women in the world's richest gold camp. More money could be made here than in any parlor house in the country.

If anything, Molly had noticed, the women curried Pearl's favor, probably hoping that they would be allowed to stay here long enough to accumulate a great sum of money. While they were the *crème de la crème,* each woman was a realist, aware that youthful beauty passes. A fortune earned today meant security, perhaps a life of ease, tomorrow.

Later in the afternoon, Winfield Shaw's top buggy arrived at the rear entrance of the Old Homestead. The driver, Molly noticed by daylight, was armed with a revolver in his waistband and a lever-action rifle in the seat beside him. He drove Molly to Bennett and the Cripple Creek Bank.

She climbed the stairs to the second floor and walked down the hallway to Clint's office. The moment before she rapped on the door, she heard low and intense voices inside.

Her knock was answered by Clint. He seemed surprised to see her in the moment before Shaw stepped into view. The millionaire wore a plain dark suit and vest — no gold watch chain or other trappings of wealth. He cast a faint smile at Molly.

"I sent for her, Clint," he said. "Or rather,

she sent word through Pearl that it was important she see me." To Molly, he said, "Come in, come in."

Molly entered the office, sensing that she had interrupted a difference of opinion, if not an outright dispute, between the two men.

She gave a detailed report to Winfield Shaw, while Clint sat on the edge of his desk, looking on. Both men were amazed to learn that Candace was dead and listened intently while Molly advanced her theory about Candace being murdered.

She wondered if they would come to the same conclusion about Luckett that she had. But neither did. Like Marshal Broyles, they accepted the death of a prostitute in a Myers Avenue crib as an unfortunate fact of life.

Molly took the money that remained of the five hundred dollars out of her handbag. When she held it out to Shaw, he waved her away.

"Keep that as a bonus," he said, "and accept my apologies. I doubted that you could do the job, and now I wish I'd kept my thoughts to myself. Even if that woman hadn't died, you'd have cleared up this case in about forty-eight hours from the time you got off the train. I'll send a letter of commendation to Horace Fenton."

"Thank you," Molly said, but as she spoke, her words sounded hollow. The real job was unfinished.

"Now if you would solve our labor problems, Molly," Clint said with half a smile.

"What sort of problems?" she asked, turning to him. Their eyes met and held for a moment.

"Now, now," Shaw said. "No need to drag anyone else into this, Clint. I've made up my mind."

Obviously exasperated, Clint said, "He wants to meet with that outlaw Riley Newcomb. The mine owners will run Win out of the Cripple Creek district tarred and feathered if he goes through with it."

"I'm not the man who's causing the problem," Shaw said with a trace of anger in his voice. "When the miners get wind of this harebrained plan to go from eight-hour shifts to nine hours with no raise in wages, they'll strike. I'm trying to head it off, that's all."

Clint shook his head as though he'd been over this point a dozen times. "Once you open the door to those union outlaws, you'll never get it closed."

The two stared at one another, neither blinking.

At last, Shaw turned to Molly. "Thanks again for your help, Miss Owens."

Taking that as her cue to leave, Molly went to the door. Clint overtook her and pulled the door open for her.

"Good-by, Molly," he said.

She smiled and nodded once. "Clint."

As their eyes met, Molly again felt stirred by this man. He was roughly handsome, but more than looks, he possessed an aura of power and strength. He was certain of himself without being arrogant, and Molly found herself regretting that she would not see him again.

In the Old Homestead that evening, Molly changed to a long dress with a tight bodice and low neckline and combed out her long blonde hair. She left her room and walked down the narrow hall to the door of the front parlor.

The pianist was playing "My Old Kentucky Home" as she entered the dimly lighted room. Once her eyes adjusted to the dim light, she saw several men in the room. Some were seated with Pearl's girls, but others sat together in pairs and threes, smoking cigars and talking.

Pearl crossed the room and came to Molly's side. She was dressed in her usual splendor, wearing a silk dress decorated with beads, pearls around her ample neck, pearls dangling from her ears, and more on her fingers. The neckline revealed a deep cleavage between her full breasts.

"Molly, oh, Molly," Pearl said, looking her over, "if you ever decide to change your line of work, I'd love to give you a room upstairs."

Molly smiled. "That's the best offer I've had in a long time, Pearl."

"I suppose you'll be returning to Denver soon," Pearl said.

"Yes," Molly said. "I'll catch the train tomorrow."

"I'm sad about the way things ended up," Pearl said, "even though I'm glad Win is out from under that damned lawsuit." She paused. "Molly, I hope you've forgotten that wild idea you had about Lucky."

"Is he here tonight?" Molly asked.

"No," Pearl said just as a man called to her. Glancing at the man seated on a sofa in a far corner of the parlor, she hastily whispered, "Banker from the Springs, probably wants to pay for your services."

Molly watched the big woman move across the room to the man. He beckoned by waving a long, thick cigar, and the glowing coal on the end of it inscribed red arcs in the pale light of the room.

Molly left the room and went into the gambling parlor where for the next hour and a half she helped pour champagne for the guests and played roulette. Pearl's girls came and went as men purchased fifty-dollar brass chips and took the women of their choice upstairs. At the end of the evening, the chips would be turned in to Pearl; the number of them determined each girl's earnings for the night.

"I'm getting damned tired of explaining why I can't sell a chip for you, Molly," Pearl said as she came up to her later in the evening.

Molly laughed. "Do you want me to leave?"

"Hell, no," Pearl said in a low voice. "You're stirring up these men, and that's good for business." She added, "But don't think you're going to work around here without getting paid."

"I'm paying you back for letting me use the room," Molly said. She did not tell her the real reason she was here. She wanted to see Luckett.

Half an hour later, Molly heard her name spoken, and she turned to see Clint Lange. He smiled as he greeted her.

"I want to speak to you — privately," he

said, "about doing another job for Win."

Molly nodded. "Come to my room." She put her arm through his, and they crossed the room to the door that opened into the hallway.

Clint pulled the door open. Just as they passed through, he nearly collided with another man.

"Excuse me, sir," Clint said.

Molly did not get a look at the man until she had turned and started down the hall with Clint. She glanced over her shoulder. Standing back there in the doorway was Leroy Luckett, glaring at her.

CHAPTER XI

After turning up the gas lamp, Molly closed the door and showed Clint to the settee. She sat across from him on the upholstered chair.

"What sort of job does Mr. Shaw have in mind?" she asked.

Clint paused before answering, almost shyly, and searched for words. "Well, the truth is, Molly, he doesn't have any job in mind for you. This is all my idea."

"Oh?" Molly asked.

Clint nodded. "I manage Win's business affairs here in Cripple Creek, but more than that, I'm a trouble-shooter for him." He paused again while he studied her. "I think you can help me."

"In what way?" she asked.

He glanced around the room, his eyes lingering a moment on the portrait of a nude woman emerging from a misty forest. Caught in midstride with brown hair flowing to her shoulders, she was voluptuous, with ripe breasts capped by pink nipples and rounded hips.

"I got to thinking," Clint said, looking at Molly again, "that you're in a position to hear news I might not learn until it's too late."

"Too late?" Molly asked. "You mean labor troubles, don't you?"

Clint nodded. "In the next week or ten days, the mine owners will make their announcement. I don't know what will happen when they do, but I want to be ready for trouble."

"What would you want me to do?" she asked.

"Keep your eyes and ears open," Clint said. "If I knew exactly how the miners planned to react, I might be able to prevent bloodshed."

"You want me to spy," Molly said.

Clint nodded again but said nothing.

"The Old Homestead isn't exactly a gathering place for miners and union organizers," Molly said.

"But other places down here on Myers are," Clint said. "If you could get into the Bull's-eye Saloon, you'd be right in the center of things."

Molly remembered seeing the Bull's-eye a few doors down from the Gold Coin Club.

The place was little more than a large hall with a bar and gambling tables.

"I take it that I would report to you," Molly said, "without Mr. Shaw's knowledge."

"Win will find out eventually, I suppose," Clint said, "but if I tell him now, he'll veto the idea."

Molly considered this job offer. Her first instinct was to accept. Not only was the job the sort of challenge she liked, but it would give her time to investigate the death of Candace Smith.

But she felt uncomfortable about keeping the secret from Winfield Shaw. She well knew that he and Clint were in disagreement about how best to handle the coming labor dispute, and she did not want to get caught in the middle of it. On the other hand, she trusted Clint and did not doubt that he was loyal to Shaw.

"All right, Clint," Molly said. "I'll work for you on a daily basis — on one condition."

Clint smiled. "Name it."

"I won't lie to Mr. Shaw," she said. "If he asks me what I'm doing in Cripple Creek, I'll tell him."

"Fair enough," Clint said.

"And I don't know how much longer

Pearl will let me stay here," Molly said.

"I've already explained the situation to her," Clint said. "You can stay here as long as you need to."

Now Molly was surprised. "I see you've done some groundwork."

"I like to be sure of my ground," he said, smiling. "As sure as I can be under the circumstances."

As they gazed at one another, Molly again felt stirred by this man. He had an appealing way about him, a quiet strength and forcefulness that she liked. She felt a quickening sensation seep through her and thought of another good reason to accept this job.

"We need to decide the best way for you to report to me," Clint said, leaning forward. "You can come to my office after hours —"

"Or," Molly said, gesturing around the room, "you can come to mine."

Clint grinned suddenly, then said, "But people will think . . ." His voice trailed off.

"Clint, a long time ago I quit worrying about what people think of me," Molly said. "My father used to tell me that no one in this world can pin a reputation on me, good or bad. A reputation is earned, and I'm the one who earns it."

"Your father must have been quite a man," Clint said.

"He was," Molly said softly. "The older I get, the more I realize that."

After agreeing on a time to meet again, Molly let Clint out the rear door of the Old Homestead. She walked back down the hall and went into the gambling parlor.

Standing alone at the bar was Leroy Luckett. He watched Molly cross the room.

"Either I'm not good enough for you," he said when she came to the bar beside him, "or my money isn't. Which is it?"

"Neither," Molly said with a smile.

"But you have time for a big shot like Clint Lange," he said.

"I've got time to talk to an old friend," Molly said. "We met in Denver a long time ago. Clint isn't my customer. I'm not here for that kind of work."

"Then just what the hell are you here for?" he demanded.

Molly paused. "I do have a reason."

Luckett stared at her in silent suspicion.

"I haven't told anyone," she said, "but I will tell you if you promise to keep it to yourself."

"What're you talking about?" he asked.

"You've got to promise," she said.

"Hell," he said, "I'm a busy man. I'm not

going to be spreading talk I've heard from you."

"You might," Molly said, ignoring his condescending tone, "if you knew how my work affected yours."

"What?" he said.

"I'm in Cripple Creek for one purpose," she said, "and that's to start a new business here on Myers Avenue."

"Business," Luckett repeated.

Molly nodded. "I sold everything out in Denver, collected debts, and I've brought enough cash to build the biggest sporting house in Cripple Creek."

Luckett's eyes widened. "Does Pearl know about this?"

"Not yet," Molly said.

"Just what kind of establishment do you have in mind?" he asked.

Molly glanced around the room. "A plush gambling parlor ten times the size of this one, a saloon, and rooms upstairs. All in a brick building."

"How many rooms?" he asked.

"Forty to fifty," Molly said.

Luckett stared at her. "You're serious," he said in a low voice.

"I am," Molly said. "I have the cash and the connections to make this thing work. And the prices will be right, so any working man in clean clothes can come in. Let Pearl cater to the bosses and mine owners. I'll take the working men." She added with a smile, "There's more of them."

Luckett returned the smile but clearly was thinking of something else. After a moment, he said, "You'll need a partner — a man."

Molly shook her head.

"You will," Luckett insisted. "I know this business. Mix gambling and liquor with women and you need muscle. I can hire men who are ready to use their fists or their guns. You'll need men like that, and you'll need a man who can boss them."

"Maybe you're right," Molly said.

"I know I'm right," Luckett said.

"Well, the first thing I have to do is buy some property on Myers," she said. "After that, we'll talk about a partnership."

Luckett's eyes narrowed. "So that's where Clint Lange comes into the picture. He's done a lot of land work for Shaw."

Molly smiled, letting him come to that conclusion. She ordered a glass of white wine from the bartender, and Luckett's glass was refilled with bourbon.

"Here's to success," he said, holding his glass up. Molly tipped her goblet against it, making a musical *clink*. "Success," she murmured, remembering a remark she'd once heard from Charley Castle: "If you're going to con someone, do it big. Give the sucker plenty to think about."

Later in the evening, after Luckett had returned to his Gold Coin Club, Molly stood at the edge of the crowd clustered around the roulette wheel when Pearl joined her.

"You decided to stay?" she asked with a sly smile.

Molly nodded. "I understand you and Clint had all this worked out behind my back."

Pearl laughed softly and took her aside. "I'm glad you're staying in Cripple Creek to work on Win's behalf. He needs help — more than he knows."

CHAPTER XII

The next day, Molly wired a message to the Fenton Investigative Agency, giving a full report to her employer and advising Horace Fenton that she would stay in Cripple Creek a few more days. Then, shortly before noon, she returned to Myers Avenue and walked into the Bull's-eye Saloon.

Heads turned as the bat-wing doors flapped behind her, and Molly quickly realized that no woman was expected, at least not at this early hour.

The men in the cavernous saloon who looked at her were townsmen and miners lined up elbow to elbow at the bar. A sign on the front window advertised a FREE LUNCH, but Molly knew that meant snacks of peanuts and jerky, heavily salted to make men thirsty for beer.

She strode across the sawdust-covered floor, returning the stares of the dozen or fifteen men at the bar. The saloonkeeper came to the near end of the bar to meet her, drying his hands on the soiled apron tied above his bulging belly. He wore baggy trousers, a white shirt with sleeve garters, and he smiled at Molly, raising his shaggy moustache as he did so.

"I'm looking for Mr. Hank Gibbs," Molly said. She had been told by Pearl that Gibbs owned the Bull's-eye and would probably be working behind the bar.

"Lady, you're looking directly at him," he said, ignoring the guffaws from his customers. He added, "None of these yokels ever heard me called 'Mister.' "

Molly said, "I'd like to speak to you privately."

A man at the bar hooted. He wore flannel trousers held up by wide, red suspenders and a flannel shirt. A wide-brimmed felt hat was shoved back on his head.

Gibbs cast a stern look at him, then said to Molly, "I reckon that can be arranged." He took off his apron and moved down the bar. Without warning, he threw the damp apron at the miner who had hooted, hitting him in the face. The others laughed.

Gibbs came out from behind the bar and took Molly to the rear of the saloon into a back hallway. One side of the hall was lined with kegs of beer, two high. Halfway down, on the other side, was a door that Gibbs unlocked and opened.

Inside, Molly saw a cluttered office, lighted only by a dirty window that doubled as a broom and mop closet. Dead flies littered the sill. The saloon was cleaner than the owner's office, Molly realized as she entered.

Gibbs rolled a high-backed office chair out from behind his desk for Molly, then shoved a heap of papers back on the desk top and sat on the space he had cleared.

"I can guess why you're here, ma'am," he said.

"You can?" Molly asked.

Gibbs nodded. "You're looking for your runaway husband. He came to Cripple Creek to seek his fortune, and you haven't heard from him since. You want to know if I've seen him. Bring a photograph of him?"

"I'm here on business," Molly said.

"Then you want to pay me for information about your runaway husband," Gibbs said.

"I want to know if you would consider selling the Bull's-eye Saloon," Molly said. "And, no, I don't have a husband, runaway or any other kind."

Gibbs' face registered surprise. "Sell the Bull's-eye?"

"Have you considered it?" Molly asked.

"Sure," Gibbs said. "I think about it every night when my back aches and my feet hurt and some drunk has tried to kill me."

"What's your price?" she asked.

Gibbs' shaggy moustache twitched. "Why does a pretty lady like you want to buy this joint?"

"If I have your asking price," Molly asked, "does it matter?"

"I reckon not," Gibbs said slowly. "Who do you represent?"

"Me," she said.

He rubbed his jaw thoughtfully. "Never come across a deal like this, a woman wanting to buy a saloon."

"I want the building, Mr. Gibbs," Molly said with a smile.

"Oh, I get it," Gibbs said. "You'll be doing something here besides selling mugs of beer."

Molly nodded.

Gibbs fell silent, then slapped his hands together. "I'll need to do some pencil figuring before I can give you a price."

"All right, Mr. Gibbs," Molly said, standing. "I'll come back in a day or two, and we'll talk again." She held her hand out.

Gibbs shook her hand as he came off his desk. He opened the door for her. "Sorry, I had you pegged wrong, ma'am. I thought sure you were hunting a husband. Women come to me all the time with sob stories about their men. Cripple Creek draws dreamers like honey draws flies."

"I'm counting on that," Molly said as she moved past him and went into the hallway.

Out in the saloon, she handed Gibbs a twenty-dollar gold piece. "Set up the bar," she said, and left with the men calling after her.

"Hey, lady, thanks!"

"What's your hurry?"

"Lemme return the favor, lady!"

During the next two days, Molly made similar inquiries in eighteen saloons and gambling halls on Myers. Working from a list of property owners in the city directory, she spoke to owners and managers, and in every saloon she bought a round of drinks. The rumor mill was soon running at full speed, and by the third day she could come and go in the saloons popular with miners. With Hank Gibbs and the others, she negotiated in vague terms while spending money freely.

On Saturday afternoon of that week, Myers was crowded and noisy, taking on a circus atmosphere with barkers standing at saloon doors and in front of dance halls exhorting passers-by to come in to see the ladies and sample the delights and to make their fortunes at the tables.

Molly joined the crowds on the boardwalks, hearing the clashing sounds of shouts and music. A brass band blasted away in one of the larger saloons, forcing barkers on either side of the establishment to shout even louder. The swarming crowd spilled out on to the street in places, making men and women dodge buggys, wagons, and saddle horses as well as sidestepping manure.

Judging by their dress, the men represented all professions and walks of life. Some were well-dressed professional men, but most were miners and construction workers. These men, now looking for ways to spend a week's wages, were hungry and thirsty at this hour. Others that Molly saw were poorly dressed, like the men she'd seen standing by saloon doors, jobless miners who were walking the street to be with their own kind, alert for news of work.

The women were the loudest. Dressed garishly, some were no more than girls who hid their youth beneath layers of powder and bright red rouge. They worked the boardwalks, calling out to the passing men as they attempted to drum up

111

business for the brothels.

"Hey, mister, looking for soft thighs? Come and get a juicy woman, mister, best in Cripple Creek down at Lottie's. Fat or thin, short or tall, we've got 'em all, and they're hot and wild, mister. Come down to Lottie's for something warm and wet. The best in Cripple Creek is down at Lottie's."

On the boardwalk ahead, Molly saw three girls stop a well-dressed man. While two of them kept him busy with chatter and suggestive touches, the third slipped behind him, raised the tail of his frock coat, and skillfully picked his pocket.

When the girl darted away with his wallet in hand, the other two abruptly broke off their teasing and left him standing there with a look of smiling confusion on his face.

In the evening, Molly met Clint in her room at the Old Homestead. Over a glass of brandy, she brought him up to date on her work. She had heard union talk among miners, and the name of Riley Newcomb came up frequently, as he was associated with higher wages.

Clint listened as she described her pending negotiations with various saloon men, then said, "You'll have everyone in town believing you're the wealthiest woman in Colorado."

"Right now, I'm about the brokest," she said, telling him of her habit of buying drinks for the house in most of the saloons on Myers.

"I'll give you some cash," Clint said. "Will two thousand dollars be enough?"

"That'll be enough to tempt me to abscond," she said.

Clint chuckled. "I don't want you to leave." Molly smiled and raised her brandy snifter to him.

"As a matter of fact," Clint went on, "when I asked you to stay in Cripple Creek, I had another motive in mind." He fell silent, looking at her.

Molly said, "When I accepted the job, I had another motive in mind, too."

He leaned toward her, and Molly met him halfway. They kissed, softly at first, then passionately as they moved into an embrace.

"You're a lot of woman, Molly," he said as he held her.

"I want you, Clint," Molly whispered. "I want you."

CHAPTER XIII

With the gas lamp turned out, they undressed in the near darkness of the room. Molly dropped her underclothes at her feet and came to Clint.

She reached out and touched his shoulders, then felt the firm pectoral muscles of his chest. He put his warm hands on her breasts, and her nipples came erect.

Molly ran her hands smoothly over his taut stomach. She continued stroking the entire length of Clint, enjoying a tickling sensation of hairs in the palm of her hand.

Clint whispered her name and began massaging her soft, delicately heavy breasts, and then he moved closer and wrapped his arms around her. He pulled her to him and kissed her, probing with his tongue.

In their embrace, Molly held him fast, feeling her breasts press against his powerful chest. She caressed his back, feeling his flexing muscles when he thrust against her.

They moved to the bed. Molly threw back the cover and slid in between the cool sheets, holding them open for him. He groped toward her.

"Come to me, Clint," she said.

Molly stretched her legs out as he came down on top of her. He kissed her, his breath hot with aroused desire, and then moved downward as he explored her smooth body with his lips.

She felt his mouth close over her erect nipple, and she was stirred by mounting passion at the wonderful pulling sensation of his sucking. She grasped his head and pulled him into the soft pillow of her breast. A moment later, her breath quickened when he slid his hand over the slight curve of her belly.

Clint raised up, kissed her again, and gained position between her thighs. She arched her back to receive him and guided him inside.

With slow movements, he began his thrusts inside her, moving powerfully to full depth, back then forward again. With building speed, he thrust into her again and again.

Molly felt a wonderfully molten sensation

as she held him in her thighs. Desire flaming now, she tightened her grip while he moved faster and faster, stronger and stronger, his breath hot on the side of her head and neck. Then the length of his body was wracked by spasms as he came with a warm burst, and she cried out softly in the throes of her own flowering orgasm. She held him as the sheer joy of it rippled through her body and her whole consciousness like a warm tide.

He lay on top of her, his large body now wet and pleasantly heavy. For a long while, they lay still in a silent rapture, with only the sounds of their quiet breathing. At last, he withdrew and rolled over on his back.

By the faint light in the room, she looked at his profile, the angle of his nose, jut of his jaw, and the delicate curves of his lips and chin.

He turned to her. "You're more woman than I dreamed you were."

"You dreamed about me?" she asked.

He murmured that he had.

"Dreamed what?" Molly asked.

"This," Clint said. "Only not as good."

"Takes two to be good at this," she said.

Clint chuckled. "You sure know how to make a bachelor lonely."

Molly got up and lit a candle on the washstand. Moving to the table by the settee, she poured a finger of brandy into each of the snifters and brought them to the bed. Handing one to him, she sat cross-legged on top of the blanket, seeing him look at her by the faint light of the candle. She reached out and ran her hand along his body, sliding gently over taut skin.

After a sip of brandy, Molly asked, "How did you come to work for Winfield Shaw?"

"That's one long story," Clint said. He sat up in bed, propping the pillow behind him. "I was raised by my father on our cattle ranch outside of Colorado Springs. I was in college in Denver when some Englishman quietly bought up all the land and water rights around us and forced my father to sell out."

He paused while he drank from the snifter. "My father died shortly afterward, and I drifted around, bankrolled by the inheritance. I used it to start law school in Denver but had to quit when the money ran out. I drifted around, cowboyed, worked construction, and ended up back where I started. Win Shaw had done some carpentry work for my father years ago, and late one night we crossed trails in a back-street saloon. One thing led to another, and I ended up managing some of his business affairs. Win doesn't have a head for business.

He sent me back to Denver to finish law school, and I've worked for him ever since I graduated." Clint added with a sardonic grin, "Saved me from a misspent youth, Win did."

His gaze swept over the curves and folds of her body, from her hanging breasts capped by large nipples to the fleecy blonde hair in her crotch. He reached out and touched the silken skin on the insides of her thighs, sliding his fingertips to those soft hairs between her legs, clustered there like an ivory cloud.

"I want to know everything about you, Molly," he said. "Tell me."

"There isn't much to tell, Clint," she said, smiling.

"Start at the beginning," he said.

"Well, I was born," she said, laughing. But her thoughts went to her family, and in this sexual afterglow, memories surged through her mind.

"My younger brother and I learned to fend for ourselves after our parents were killed in a railroad accident," she said. "My brother, Chick, was adventurous, and as soon as he was old enough, he came out West to work on a ranch. About that time, I learned that the Fenton Investigative Agency had jobs for single women who were willing to travel, so I went to New York and applied. I got the job, and after my training, I was stationed in Denver. Been there ever since."

Her thoughts went to the murder of her brother by a rogue town marshal and her investigation that had resulted in Charley Castle's coming to her aid. He'd saved her life.

"You like your work, don't you?" Clint asked.

Molly nodded, looking at him in the soft candlelight. She leaned across the bed and kissed him.

On Gold Hill the next day, three of the largest mines in the district, none owned by Winfield Shaw, posted notices. Shifts would increase from eight to nine hours, with no raise in wages. This was necessary, the notices read, due to severe deflation and generally declining economic conditions throughout the country.

After work, miners congregated in their favorite saloons. Their mood reminded Molly of the eerie quiet before a storm when the sky is black, all is still, but the air is charged.

The men were angry but at a loss about what they should, or could, do. Hundreds of skilled hard-rock miners from recently closed silver mines in Leadville and Aspen had swarmed into the Cripple Creek district, looking for work. If the employed miners went out on strike now, the owners would simply hire new crews from this idle labor force.

Molly listened as the answer to this predicament came in booming oratory delivered by a small, bespectacled man wearing clean work clothes and new boots. He was Riley Newcomb.

CHAPTER XIV

Molly pushed through the bat-wing doors of the Bull's-eye Saloon late in the afternoon. Miners, a few young women, and men from town jammed the saloon from the long bar to the far wall. They listened intently to Riley Newcomb, who addressed them while standing on a chair he'd pulled back from a faro table.

"Two choices are open to you men. You can blast rock and shovel muck nine hours for three dollars, six days a week for the rest of your lives . . . the rest of your lives." He looked around the room, the thick lenses of his spectacles magnifying his eyeballs and making his expression appear all the more intense.

"The mine owners will never raise your wages," he went on. "If anything, they'll cut back again. A year from now, two years from now, you men will be working ten hours a day for the same three dollars you earned by your sweat today."

"Never!" shouted a red-bearded miner in the crowd. "Never!"

Others joined in protest, shouting, "No!"

"And just what the hell are you going to do about it?" Riley Newcomb asked, raising his hand for quiet. "When the mine owners post the next notice for ten-hour shifts, what are you men going to do about that? Complain? Drink your beer and go back to work? You've already let the owners get away with shoving nine hours down your throats."

"Not yet, we haven't!" shouted a miner.

"Damned right, we ain't," called out another.

"Of the two choices," Newcomb said, "I can see you don't think much of the first one." He paused. "Well, the second choice is rougher, a lot rougher. It'll take courage, stamina, guts — all the guts you working men have. You'll have to take care of each other, help feed each other's children, stick together when you have no hope. Your second choice will bring the roughest times any man here has ever seen."

He paused again while he looked over the crowd, and a faint smile came to his face. "The only men who'll have it rougher will be the mine owners."

A cheer went up from the men.

"The mine owners won't be able to send their sons and daughters to Europe for a summer holiday," he said.

The miners cheered again.

"The mine owners won't be able to buy their mistresses another diamond necklace," Newcomb said sadly.

Hooting, the miners cheered their approval.

"But here's what they will do," Newcomb said. "They'll try to bust you. They'll try everything from beatings to bribes to bust you wide open!" He paused. "Are you men going to let the rich mine owners bust your strike?"

"No!" they shouted in unison. That word was the one they had waited to hear. They repeated it in a shouting chant.

"Strike! Strike! Strike!"

After a few moments, Newcomb signaled for quiet. When the shouts died down, he spoke in a low tone of voice. "It's one thing to talk strike, but it's something else when you're eating two meals a day of pinto beans and sowbelly, knowing all the while that some bastard is working your shift in the mine."

The men in the saloon grew still.

"We all know plenty of men are looking

for work in this district," he said quietly. "And somebody might be wondering how we can strike when all the owners have to do to fill out a crew is post a sign that says HIRING. Somebody might be wondering about that."

Riley Newcomb placed his hands on his hips. "The answer is easy, so damned easy that it scares every rich exploiter who ever breathed. The answer is this: find those out-of-work men and bring them into the union. Unite. Every man among you, unite." Voice rising, he said, "Unite, and you'll bust the richest bastards in the country!"

The men cheered and waved their hats in the air, intoxicated by the feeling of power that swept over them. Newcomb stepped down from the chair, and miners pressed forward, swarming around him, shouting triumphantly.

Molly watched this scene, impressed by the way Riley Newcomb had handled the crowd and rallied these men to his cause. He was a man small in stature but large in presence and clearly a dynamic leader. The miners would follow him. She had no doubt of that.

Throughout the afternoon, she watched and listened as Newcomb preached his message from one crowded saloon on Myers

Avenue to another, followed by two of his workers, who handed out leaflets to passers-by on the boardwalks.

UNITE AGAINST
THE RICH MINE OWNERS!
DON'T BE EXPLOITED!
STRIKE!

In the evening, Molly gave her report to Clint. He stood in the middle of her room in the Old Homestead, arms folded across his chest, a grim expression lining his brow.

"It's an old trick," Clint said. "Stir the workers up, then unite them behind a cause. He'll have his strike, looks like."

Molly felt troubled. "Clint, why did those three mine owners add an hour to the shifts?"

"Losing money, they claim," Clint replied. "They want to ship more gold ore."

"Are they losing money," Molly asked, "or making less profit than they want?"

Clint shrugged. "Only their accountants could tell you that."

"But Mr. Shaw isn't losing money on his properties, is he?" Molly asked.

"Win's ground on Gold Hill is so rich," Clint said, "that he leaves ore in the mines so his daily income won't exceed three

125

thousand dollars." He added, "But if he doesn't go along with the nine-hour shifts, the other mine owners will make life hard for him. They might even shut down the railroad so no one can ship ore."

Molly thought a moment, then asked, "What's next?"

"Any investigating you can do down here on Myers will be helpful," Clint said. He came to her and put his hands on her shoulders. "But be careful. Newcomb has these men fired up, and there may be violence once this strike gets going."

She nodded, and he leaned down and kissed her briefly.

Clint moved to the door. "I'll advise Win to wire the governor tonight. We may need the state militia to prevent bloodshed." He put his hand on the door handle and said over his shoulder, "If you hear anything new, get word to me."

"I will," Molly replied.

She stared absently at the closed door for several moments after Clint was gone. She had a terrible feeling that they were all being sucked into something, a small war perhaps, because of the actions of three mine owners.

Molly wondered what Leroy Luckett's slant on all this was. He was shrewd and knew men on both sides of this dispute.

Restless, she put on a wrap, picked up her handbag, and left the Old Homestead through the back door. The cool night was lighted by half a moon. Countless stars were sprinkled across the night sky like sugar crystals.

Molly walked out of the back alley to Myers. The street was nearly empty when she angled across it toward the Gold Coin Club. Night sounds from the saloon district drifted to her: tinkling music from upright pianos, occasional shouts mixed with laughter, singing that was far off key.

Molly stepped up on the boardwalk, not seeing a shadowy figure there until too late.

Lunging out of the darkness, a man grabbed her from behind. He yanked her off her feet, slapping one rough hand over her mouth.

"Don't holler," he growled as he dragged her into the darkness between two buildings. He stomped through a pile of trash and rusting cans, setting Molly down. He took his hand away from her mouth and threw his forearm around her neck, tightening his grip on her throat.

"I've seen you around here, lady. You look like you've got money." With his free hand, he reached for the handbag hanging from her shoulder.

"Let me go," Molly said hoarsely, "and we'll forget this ever happened."

"What?" he asked with a harsh laugh. "Just what the hell you aim to do about it, lady?" He drew his forearm back until Molly could not breathe, then cupped a hand over her breast. "Now just what the hell you gonna do?"

Molly shifted her weight to one side. She stuck her leg out in front of her, leaned back against her attacker, and brought the heel of her high-button shoe back against his shin.

The man howled, and his grip loosened slightly. Molly gasped, lowered her head, and butted it back. She banged him again, and his arm fell away from her throat.

Grasping his wrist with both hands, Molly thrust it straight out and stepped under it. She gave his arm a downward snap. The man's body flipped end over end. He landed flat on his back, hard.

Molly breathed deeply, filling her lungs, until her attacker moaned and slowly turned over. He raised to all fours, head hanging down. Molly moved behind him, placed her foot on his tail bone, and shoved. The man sprawled forward, clattering into the heap of trash.

"What's going on there?" came a deep

voice from the boardwalk. "My gun's on you. Come out!"

By moonlight, Molly saw the burly figure of a man, and she recognized the voice of Marshal Broyles.

"This man assaulted me, marshal," Molly said, stepping around the prone figure on the trash heap. She came out to the boardwalk where Broyles stood with a large revolver in his hand. The badge on his dark coat reflected moonlight.

Molly went on, "I was walking along here, and he lunged out and grabbed me, forced me back in there, and tried to rob me."

Broyles grunted and moved past her, holstering the revolver. He dragged the man out of the darkened space between the two buildings to the boardwalk. The marshal turned the dazed man's face to the moonlight.

"Robbing women now, are you, Pinky?" Broyles demanded.

The man's head lolled from side to side. Broyles turned to Molly. "I've run him in before, ma'am, but he's never tried anything like this — not that I know of. Must have got himself drunked up before he tried robbing you. He's harmless enough now."

Marshal Broyles cast a second look at Molly. "Say, you're —"

"Molly Owens," she said.

"Sure, I remember you," he said, straightening up to face her. "What're you doing out this time of night, all alone?"

"I was on my way to see Mr. Luckett."

"Sure, now," he interrupted. "I've been hearing talk about you, Molly Owens. You're the one who's buying up property down here on Myers. What's your game?"

"No game, marshal," Molly said. She was irritated by his blunt questioning, but at the same time she sensed his suspicion of her. "Business."

"What sort of business?" he asked.

"Nothing against the law," she replied.

Broyles studied her, then said, "You'll be out of business permanent if you wander around here after dark."

Molly did not point out the obvious fact that she could take care of herself, a fact illustrated by Pinky's swollen nose and cheek where she had hammered him with the back of her head. She let the marshal believe that her assailant had been too drunk to be dangerous.

"Thanks for the advice," she said as Broyles stooped down and lifted Pinky to his feet. Molly watched while the big lawman handcuffed her attacker and took him away.

CHAPTER XV

Since her arrival, Molly had become aware that the establishments on Myers Avenue represented all layers of Cripple Creek society, from the raucous nickel beer halls with sawdust-covered floors to the quiet elegance and thickly carpeted floors of the Old Homestead. The saloons, dance halls, gambling parlors, brothels, and cribs all catered to certain clientele, from the fattened to the hungry.

No one was hungry in the Gold Coin Club. As Molly stepped inside, she saw that it was a small, quiet place, more of a gentlemen's meeting room and gambling parlor than a drinking establishment. Leather upholstered chairs were clustered around tables of polished walnut, and in the back of the room were three felt-covered gaming tables, a roulette wheel, and an upright piano, now silent.

The men there were dressed in suits, and

they all turned to stare at the lone woman who had entered their domain. Molly returned their stares as she moved to the small bar fronting an elaborate back bar with long, vertical mirrors. Between the mirrors were wooden pillars carved in the Corinthian style. Coming around the bar to meet her was Leroy Luckett.

"Well, well," he said, "to what do I owe the honor of this visit? Have you come to buy my club?"

Molly smiled even though she clearly heard the rancor in his voice. "Is this property for sale?"

He did not reply but glared at her. "You've been busy since I last saw you, mighty busy. You've tipped off everyone in town that you're looking for property. By now, you can bet prices have gone up on sheer speculation. Have you been taking Clint Lange's advice?"

Molly was unprepared for his verbal onslaught. "I'm here to ask your advice," she said.

He glared at her. "Follow me."

She followed him through the club to a short hallway in the rear. Molly entered the hall, lighted by gas lamps, behind Luckett, watching him draw a key from his vest pocket. He stopped at a door and inserted the key into the lock below the brass handle. He unlocked the door and went in, turning up a lamp.

Molly saw that the decor in the office was in keeping with the masculine atmosphere of the club.

The walls were paneled with walnut. A roll-top desk was on the far wall, along with a caned swivel chair.

In the middle of the room on a multi-colored Persian carpet were leather uphol-stered chairs grouped around a low table. A cut-glass decanter and glasses were on a tray there.

In a far corner of the room, Molly saw a large safe, black with nickel-plated hinges and lever-type handle. On the safe door, within a painted gold frame, was a fanciful mountain scene depicting a waterfall and lush forest under a blue sky filled with white clouds that looked like tufts of cotton.

After she was seated in one of the chairs, Luckett sat across from her. Without a word to her, he poured a glass of bourbon for himself. He slugged down a gulp, then leaned back in the chair, staring at Molly.

"What are you up to?" he demanded.

"Up to?" she asked.

"You aren't buying property around here," Luckett said.

"I am," Molly insisted.

He shook his head while staring at her. "No one would go about it the way you have." He added, "You're good-looking enough to keep men distracted, and I hear you've flashed money around Myers Avenue, enough money to choke a horse." He took a long swallow of bourbon and banged the glass down on the table top. "From the day we met, you've played me like a fish on a line. How many other men have you got on your line?"

"Mr. Luckett —"

"Shut up," he interrupted. He stared at her for several seconds. "Nobody plays me for a fool and gets away with it. If I wanted to find out what you're up to, I'd sure as hell do it — if I had to beat the truth out of you."

"Like you beat the truth out of Candace?" Molly asked. The question had been on her mind for days, and in the heat of the moment it practically flew out of her mouth.

"What did you say?" Luckett whispered.

Molly leaned forward, using her body movement to keep him from seeing that she slid her hand into her handbag. Her finger-tips touched the cold steel of her revolver.

"You beat up Candace," Molly said, "and she died from it."

Luckett had been angry, but now, instead

of exploding, he became reserved and distant. "You have no proof of that," he said slowly, "because it never happened. Now I suggest you leave."

Without removing her hand from her handbag, Molly stood. Luckett's gaze never left her in the time it took her to reach the door. Molly opened it and quickly stepped out into the hall, closing the door after her. Then she took a deep breath.

CHAPTER XVI

The next morning, Riley Newcomb ordered miners out of the American Eagle, Lucky Cuss, and Jackpot mines, the three whose owners had given notice for nine-hour shifts. To a man, the miners complied. Picking up their lunch buckets, they walked out, thereby removing any lingering doubts in the Cripple Creek district of Newcomb's ability to assert authority over the men.

Molly heard this news, and on Myers Avenue she saw a victorious, festive atmosphere rise up and prevail throughout the day. The saloons were filled from midmorning on. Revelers spilled drunkenly into the streets, singing songs and shouting obscene taunts at the mine owners, none of whom were in earshot.

In the evening came word that the foremen of the struck mines were hiring. Rumor spread like fire through the saloons that full crews had been assembled for the day shift in the American Eagle, Lucky Cuss, and Jackpot.

Newcomb raced from one saloon to another and organized those men who were sober enough to listen. Early in the morning, when the new crews walked up the hill to the mines, they were met by strikers armed with ax handles, brass knuckles, and a few with pistols thrust through their waistbands.

For a time, the two sides shouted curses and threats at one another, but it soon became apparent that the strikers had achieved their purpose just as Riley Newcomb had predicted. The new men wanted work, but none were willing to risk a beating to get to the job.

Her suspicion was confirmed when she answered a knock on her door that night and found Clint in the hallway. Beside him stood a somber Winfield Shaw.

Clint said with a grin, "I let Win in on our little conspiracy, Molly."

She admitted them, seeing a fleeting smile on Shaw's face as the millionaire moved past her.

"Clint has a way of knowing when to act on his own," Shaw said. "I'm glad he kept you in town. I have a job that needs to be done, and you may be the only one who can do it."

Molly showed him to the chair across the room, and she sat on the settee. Clint sat beside her.

"What job is that?" she asked.

Shaw thought a moment before answering. "Against the advice of Clint, I met secretly with Riley Newcomb. I offered to pay miners $3.50 for a nine-hour shift in the Independence and all my other properties. I felt certain that if Newcomb accepted my offer, all the owners would go along and we'd avoid trouble."

Shaw paused. He looked tired and old when he went on, "Newcomb declined my offer, and demanded $3.50 for an eight-hour shift, with no compromises."

"Arrogant bastard," Clint said.

"Still," Shaw said, taking a deep breath, "I don't want to lose contact with Newcomb. Like it or not, he has some power right now. But after today, I can't meet with him. Passions are running high, and if word got out that I was seeing the man, the strikers would go wild, and so would the mine owners."

"I say call in the troops," Clint said.

"We may have to," Shaw said. To Molly, he added, "I've notified the governor, and he's put the state militia on standby." He paused. "But in the meantime I'd like you to act as go-between with Newcomb and me. No one knows you worked for me, and you should be able to go back and forth without raising suspicions and without some hot-head taking a shot at you."

"Sounds like an armed camp," Molly said.

"From what we've heard," Shaw said, "that's exactly what you'll be riding into."

Clint added, "Newcomb has himself forted up in a cabin outside of town, and it's patrolled by guards."

"How can I get in?" Molly asked. "Newcomb doesn't know me."

Shaw became uncomfortable, and he shifted his weight in the chair and looked downward.

Molly looked questioningly at Clint. He reached into his vest pocket and drew out a brass chip from the Old Homestead.

"Tell them Pearl sent you," he said, holding the chip out to her.

"You took me at my word," Molly said, "when I told you that I never worried about my reputation, didn't you?"

Clint smiled. "You don't have to do this, Molly. Maybe you can come up with a better plan to get past the guards."

"I'm afraid I can't," Molly said. "It's a very good ruse."

Relieved, Shaw looked up and smiled briefly. "I'll see that you're well paid for this . . . embarrassment."

Molly chuckled. "Pay me as well as Pearl's girls are paid, Mr. Shaw, and I'll be real happy."

The two men laughed.

"What message do you want me to relay to Riley Newcomb?" Molly asked.

"Just tell him that I hope we can work together to avoid bloodshed," Shaw replied. "And tell him that I want to keep the lines of communication open between us. Any time he wants to get a message to me, he can send it through you."

Molly nodded. "All right."

Shaw stood, and so did Clint. Molly left the settee and showed them to the door. Clint cast a long glance back at her, and Molly nodded. In a quarter of an hour, he came back alone.

They hardly spoke as they undressed in the cold darkness of the room. In bed, they came together in a hard embrace, clinging, silently warming one another.

Molly felt a wave of heat and tingling excitement ripple through her as Clint's hands began caressing her back, exploring with his fingers down to her buttocks and inner thighs. She felt him come alive.

Clint brought his mouth to hers and kissed her long and deeply, probing her mouth with his tongue. He moved against her, stimulating her breasts with his bare chest.

Enormously aroused now, Molly moved her hands on his skin, feeling rippling muscles in his back, and reached downward until her fingertips touched downy hairs in the small of his back. She held on while he turned and moved on top of her.

Clint raised up, gained position, and lowered his body. Molly grasped him and guided him inside. He pushed in all the way, bumping against her. Pulling back, coming forward, he began his rhythmic movements. Slowly at first, much too slowly for her rising passion, he moved back and forth, gradually building speed with his powerful thrusts.

Molly's emotions soared as she held his pumping torso, climbing to a peak of dizzying excitement, and then she felt deep and delicious tremors surge through her body and through her whole consciousness as Clint's body was wracked by spasms and his warmth flowed into her.

Afterward they lay together in a silent embrace. Aware of his breathing, Molly lay against Clint. She enjoyed the peacefulness brought by their moment of complete unity, a feeling that she once thought had been lost forever.

Clint turned in the bed, laying an arm across her breasts. "I don't like the idea of your going there tomorrow. I'll follow you from a distance —" His voice trailed off.

"No, Clint," Molly said. "If Newcomb is guarded as closely as you said he was, that won't work." She looked at his shadowy face in the near darkness. "You and Winfield are in disagreement over this whole thing, aren't you?"

Clint murmured that they were. "If the decision were mine, the state militia would be here right now. We'd bust this illegal strike and run Newcomb and his outlaws out of the district before any lives are lost."

"Will it come to that?" Molly asked.

"It could," Clint said. "But I aim to stop Newcomb no matter what it takes."

CHAPTER XVII

The next evening, Molly wore a fur wrap over her shoulders and a lap robe while she drove Pearl's one-horse buggy on the road out of Cripple Creek. The day had been warm, but at this altitude the air chilled the moment the sun dropped below the mountainous horizon.

She had received directions from Clint, and now by evening light she watched for a side road two miles away from town. When she found it, she turned off the ore-wagon road on to a set of wheel ruts that curved toward a few gold mines on a low hill.

As Molly drew closer, she saw that these were small operations, three or four men working each one, probably, and now were silent. She followed the wheel ruts past mounds of oxidized soil and rock and drove over the top of the hill.

On the far side was a grass-laden valley with a creek meandering through the bottom. Down there, Molly saw what Clint had described: a squat log cabin with several slab outbuildings and a pole corral.

Driving the buggy down the sloping hillside, Molly saw that the cabin ahead had some of the attributes of a small fort. The logs were thick enough to repel bullets, and with open ground all around, riders could be seen from a considerable distance.

Movement in one of the outbuildings told her that she had been seen, and as she drew nearer, three men carrying rifles stepped into the yard in front of the cabin.

"That's close enough, lady." The man who spoke was unshaved, wearing trousers splattered with mud, a dark brown mackinaw, and a wide-brimmed black felt hat. He stepped forward while the other two men, dressed similarly, held their rifles at the ready.

Molly drew back on the reins a dozen yards away.

"What's your business?" the man asked.

Molly drew a brass chip from the Old Homestead out of her handbag. She tossed it to him. "I'm here to see Mr. Newcomb."

The man caught the chip after quickly shifting his rifle to one hand. He briefly examined it, then looked at Molly. "You ain't expected. Riley don't want you."

Molly smiled. "Don't you think he ought to be the judge of that?"

The man paused, caught in a moment of indecision. He abruptly turned and walked between the other two guards to the cabin.

After the man had gone inside and closed the door behind him, Molly saw a flash of lamplight as a curtain moved in a window. Presently, the man returned and without a word helped Molly down from the buggy. He abruptly took her handbag, opened it, and plunged his hand inside.

Molly watched him search her bag, glad that she had decided to leave her revolver behind. She was armed only with the derringer in the holster strapped to her leg.

"You can go in," the man said, thrusting the handbag out to her.

Molly took it and walked away from him, following the beaten path in the high grass to the cabin door. That door now stood partly open. In the aperture, back lighted by the pale glow of lamps, was Riley Newcomb.

"Mr. Newcomb," Molly said when she reached the door, "I'm Molly Owens."

"Come in," he said, stepping back. Molly was a foot taller, and he looked up at her when he spoke, his thick, silver-rimmed spectacles reflecting lamplight. As always, he wore work clothes that appeared to have just come off the shelf of a dry goods store.

The cabin had a dirt floor and was sparsely furnished. As Molly walked in, she saw a single bunk near one wall and a battered table and chairs in the middle of the room; near the other wall stood a sheet-iron cook stove with a counter and shelves built of rough, unpainted pine boards.

Molly turned around as Newcomb closed the door. "We're alone?" she asked.

Newcomb nodded.

"I'm not one of Pearl's girls," Molly said in a low voice. "I was sent here by Winfield Shaw."

"I suspected that," Newcomb said, "when I saw you out there in the buggy. I remember seeing you in the hall outside Lange's office a while back." He added, "I confess my disappointment, though, that you're not what you pretended to be."

Molly smiled. "You have a good memory. We saw one another only for a moment."

"You make an impression, Miss Owens," he said, "quite an impression."

Still smiling, she said, "Call me Molly." She liked this man, realizing now that he had a dry wit about him.

"All right, Molly," Newcomb said, "if

you're not here for pleasure, what can I do for you?"

"Mr. Shaw wants to stay in secret communication with you," she said, "and he's hired me as go-between."

"I see," Newcomb said. "Well, what does he have to say?"

"He wants to avoid bloodshed," Molly said, "and —"

Newcomb interrupted her with an abrupt, harsh laugh. "That's quite a statement, coming from him."

"What do you mean?" Molly asked.

Newcomb stared at her as though wondering if she meant the question sincerely. After a long moment, he said, "Ask Winfield Shaw about his hired thugs and you'll know what I mean — if you're the fair-minded person I judge you to be."

"I will ask him," Molly said. "But I'd like to hear your side of the story, too."

Newcomb considered this, then glanced toward the stove. A dented, scorched coffee pot was on it. "Care to sit down and have a cup of mud?" He added, "It's wise to be seated when you drink my brew."

Molly smiled. "I'll take you up on that."

She went to the table and sat down while Newcomb crossed the room to the stove. He took two tin cups from a shelf and filled them with steaming coffee.

Papers with scribbled notes, handbills boldly proclaiming the union message, and several newspapers were scattered across the scarred table top. Looking at Newcomb's scribbled notes, Molly realized that this sparsely furnished cabin was the heart and soul of the whole union movement in the Cripple Creek district.

She glanced around at the bare log walls and thought of the plush offices of mine owners like Winfield Shaw. Shaw and the other owners were wealthy and powerful. Molly turned and saw Newcomb coming to the table, a small man wearing clean work clothes and now carrying two cups of steaming coffee, and she thought, *Riley Newcomb doesn't stand a chance.*

He set a cup down on the table in front of Molly and took a chair across from her. He sat down, raised the tin cup to his mouth, and sipped loudly.

"Well, it's hot, anyhow," he said.

Molly took a swallow and nodded agreement. The brew was too hot to taste, and from its thick consistency she believed that was for the best.

"When I say the mine owners plan to use violence to bust the strike," Newcomb said, setting the cup down in front of him, "I know it for a fact. At this moment, thugs are being hired in Colorado Springs. A trainload of the bastards is expected in the next couple of days, three at the most."

"How do you know that?" Molly asked.

Newcomb didn't answer for a time. "Suffice it to say that some people in unlikely places are sympathetic to the miners' cause."

"You mean people in mine owners' offices?" Molly asked.

Newcomb smiled with a shrug, then said, "Listen, I don't want trouble. I don't want any man hurt. A strike doesn't have to be violent, and I've done my best to keep my men from using it. But the mine owners may not give me any choice. I won't put my men in a position where they'll be slaughtered."

"You're certain the mine owners would do that?" Molly asked.

"I am," Newcomb said. He took another loud sip of coffee. "And I know the name of the man who's hiring and arming those thugs."

"Who is he?" Molly asked.

"Leroy Luckett," Newcomb replied.

CHAPTER XVIII

"Luckett," Molly repeated, surprised to hear the name. But as she thought about it, she realized Luckett was the man for the job. He was ruthless, and his only loyalty was to money.

"Winfield Shaw wouldn't have any part of this," Molly said.

Newcomb shrugged. "Personally, I find it hard to believe Shaw is unaware of the mine owners' plans."

"He would not have any dealings with Luckett," Molly insisted. "I'm not at liberty to explain why, but I hope you'll take my word for it. I know what I'm talking about."

Newcomb studied her.

Molly went on, "I'm certain Mr. Shaw wants to avoid bloodshed. To prevent trouble, he's notified the governor, and right now the state militia is on standby."

Newcomb's eyebrows shot up, as he was obviously surprised to learn that. "The other mine owners want to settle this thing their own way, with their own men."

"That's right," Molly said. "Winfield Shaw is not your enemy. He's caught in the middle, caught between the mine owners and you."

A skeptical look returned to Newcomb's face.

Molly said, "You and Shaw have a common purpose. Why don't you work together?"

Newcomb exhaled. "I tried to work with him. I gave Shaw a chance to end this whole dispute when I offered $3.50 for an eight-hour shift. If the Independence paid that, the other mines might have gone along."

Riley Newcomb looked at Molly intently. "Did Shaw take my offer? Hell, no. All he can think about is getting richer. He should be thinking about the men who give their sweat and blood so he can bank $3,000 every day." Newcomb added, "For a man who spent most of his life working, he ought to know better."

"Perhaps he does," Molly said. "If I can convince Mr. Shaw that he should work with you for a peaceable solution, will you agree to work with him?"

Newcomb considered this, and a faint smile came to his lips. "Any man would have a hard time saying no to you." He paused. "My answer is a conditional yes."

"What are the conditions?" Molly asked.

"Just one," he said. "I won't compromise on $3.50 for an eight-hour shift."

Molly nodded. "I'll relay that to Mr. Shaw." She took a last sip of the foul coffee and stood.

Newcomb slid his chair back and got to his feet. "Winfield Shaw is not the one who's caught in the middle. You are. And you don't have much time. Some hotheaded miners around here are ready to shoot it out with anyone who gets in their way. I've been able to control them up to now, but when those hired thugs climb off the train in Cripple Creek, I can't promise protection for you or for anyone else."

"I understand that," Molly said, "and I'll try to get things moving quickly." She held out her hand to shake.

Newcomb shook hands with her. "I'll do what I can to keep my people in line. Can the famous Winfield Shaw do the same?"

The question echoed in Molly's thoughts as she drove the buggy through the gathering darkness back to Cripple Creek. In truth, she did not know if Shaw could do anything to stop the impending confrontation. Even though he was the wealthiest man here, she had sensed that he was not highly regarded by the other mine owners.

According to plan, Molly was waiting in her room in the Old Homestead when Clint and Winfield Shaw arrived through the back door. She gave her report and saw the two men exchange glances when she told them Riley Newcomb was convinced that armed strikebreakers were being hired by the mine owners.

"Newcomb claims the whole thing is being arranged by Leroy Luckett," she said.

"Luckett," Shaw growled. "That name is starting to haunt my dreams."

Clint shook his head. "Rumors about strikebreakers have been going around, but I doubt if there's anything to it."

"Newcomb is convinced it's true," Molly said. "I got the impression that he has a spy in the office of a mine owner."

"Wouldn't surprise me," Shaw said.

"This could be just another tactic of Newcomb's to put pressure on you, Win," Clint said. "He knows that if the Independence raises wages to $3.50, he'll have won a big victory."

Shaw pursed his lips in thought, then turned to Molly. "What do you think of this Newcomb character?"

"I think he's sincere when he says he doesn't want violence," she replied. "But he won't back down, and he truly believes strikebreakers are being hired. He's convinced the mine owners intend to use violence." Out of the corner of her eye, she saw Clint cast a severe glance at her.

"I still say, don't trust anything that outlaw says," Clint said.

Shaw stood. "I want to pay a visit to my so-called colleagues tonight, Clint, and get to the bottom of this thing. If what Newcomb says is true, then I'll wire the governor and tell him we need troops down here."

Shaw turned to Molly. "Stay here until I get word to you. If it's true that Lucky has been hired to bring in strikebreakers, then Newcomb will have my full cooperation."

Molly nodded and saw the two men to the door. A hard look was on Clint's face and as he passed by, he avoided looking at her.

Events moved swiftly the next day, and Molly had the dizzying sensation that everyone involved was plummeting toward disaster.

Riley Newcomb exerted his power even further by calling men out of half a dozen mines, and the new strikers ringed those properties to prevent their foremen from hiring new crews. None of these mines were owned by Winfield Shaw.

Molly spent part of the day speculating with Pearl about what would happen next and looking out the window at Myers Avenue. The miners who passed by on their way to the saloons were armed with revolvers, and a few carried shotguns and rifles.

"All the guests were talking against the strike last night," Pearl said, "but every one of my girls is secretly for it."

Molly smiled at Pearl while they considered this irony. Then came a rapping at the back door, and presently Colleen entered the front parlor.

"Mr. Lange to see you, Miss Owens," she said.

Molly met Clint in the back hallway and let him into her room. He was grim faced and did not speak until she had closed the door and turned to face him.

"Well, you did it," he said.

Molly waited for him to explain, but he continued staring at her. "What do you mean?"

"Shaw's throwing in with Newcomb," Clint said.

"Then it's true?" Molly asked. "The mine owners hired Luckett to bring in strikebreakers?"

Clint replied with a single nod of his head. He exhaled loudly. "Win wants you to carry the word to Newcomb. The Independence and all of Shaw's mines will raise wages to $3.50 for an eight-hour shift." He paused and added, "Hell's going to bust loose. I hope you're satisfied."

"Satisfied?" Molly asked.

"That's right — satisfied," he said angrily. "You're the one who convinced Win that Newcomb is such a fine, honorable fellow."

"Clint, I carried messages back and forth," Molly said. "Mr. Shaw asked me what I thought, and I told him."

"You did more than that," Clint said. "You made Newcomb sound respectable."

Molly shook her head while she met his angry glare. She found it difficult now to think of Clint as the man who had been her lover. "If I helped establish trust between two men who are suspicious of one another, have I done something wrong? You've said from the beginning that you wanted to avoid bloodshed."

"I do," Clint said, "but I won't be run over by those union outlaws. Don't you see? They want to take away the employers' right to determine wages. Free enterprise can't work that way."

"Shouldn't you be telling that to Mr. Shaw?" Molly asked. "He's the one who decided to talk to Riley Newcomb."

"Win is uneducated," Clint said, "and doesn't see the larger issue at stake. That's why he needs me to look out for his interests."

"Does he need you," Molly asked, "or do you need him?"

"What the hell do you mean by that?" Clint demanded angrily.

"Sounds to me like you want to use him to promote your own beliefs," Molly said. She met his gaze, waiting for him to reply. When he did not, she asked, "When are the strike-breakers due in Cripple Creek?"

"That's information you don't need," Clint said curtly. "Just carry the damned message to Newcomb." He turned away and moved to the door, yanked it open, and stomped out of the room. Moments later, the back door slammed like a shot.

Molly was angry, too, and saddened. Clint was gone — in more ways than one.

A quarter of an hour later, she drove Pearl's buggy to the far end of Myers and turned on to the road out of Cripple Creek, passing the weathered shacks and tents on the outskirts of town.

The day did not match her mood. The sky

157

of early afternoon was clear, a deep blue that she had seen only at these high altitudes in the Rockies, and the air was still and sun warmed, fragrant with the scent of flowers and high grass.

The road wound through a grove of white-barked aspen trees. Molly saw their light green leaves fluttering with a slight mountain breeze. Farther on, the aspen grove gave way to a pine forest, and among those trees she saw a pair of deer watching her. Standing still as statues, the does watched her pass by.

Shouts warned her that ore wagons were coming, and Molly pulled off to the side as three mule-drawn wagons came around the bend, with teamsters calling to their animals and popping whips over the lead mules. The big iron-tired vehicles raised clouds of billowing dust in their wake.

The horse pulling the buggy tossed his head at this indignity. Molly let some slack in the reins, and the horse broke into a trot, then a canter. Cool air breezed her face, and the dust cloud was left behind.

Half a mile farther, Molly reined the horse down and immediately became aware of hoofbeats behind her. An instant later, a masked horseman drew up beside the buggy. He aimed a long-barreled revolver in her face.

"Turn loose of those reins," he ordered.

On the other side of the buggy, a second horsebacker swept past. He was masked, too, with a red bandanna covering the lower part of his face. He reached out and grabbed the reins and guided the animal off the road into the pine trees.

CHAPTER XIX

The buggy bounced wildly and was raked by pine branches as the masked riders led the horse into cool shadows deep in the forest. Far out of sight of the road, one man halted the horse while the second aimed his revolver at Molly.

"Get out," he said.

Molly climbed out of the buggy and reached back in for her handbag. "If it's money you want —"

"Shut up," he said. "Don't make no moves."

Molly clutched her handbag and watched while the second man dismounted and quickly unhitched the horse from Pearl's buggy. Besides bandanna masks, both men wore long dusters that reached down to their boot tops and narrow-brimmed, low-crowned hats. One was dark haired, the other light, but beyond that, Molly could not see what either man looked like.

"If this buggy horse ain't broke for riding," the man said as he slipped a hackamore over the horse's head, "you're walking."

"Go on," said the other. "Climb up."

Molly moved to the left side of the horse, running her hand over the animal's back. She slung her handbag over her shoulder and grasped a handful of mane. The horse cocked his ears and shied, but the man held him.

Molly hopped and swung a leg over the horse's bare back. The horse quivered and laid his ears back but did not pitch. He was led a few steps and seemed to have no objection to being ridden.

Molly held on tightly to the horse's mane with both hands. Her attention was on the jittery horse, and she was only vaguely aware that the second masked rider had moved close beside her. In the next instant, he threw a flour sack over her head.

"Now don't fight it, lady," he said, punching his gun barrel into her ribs, "and you won't get hurt. Just go along."

Her nostrils and throat filled with powdery flour, making her sneeze and choke at once. The horse beneath her moved, and one of the men gave another command.

"Duck down. We're going through some trees."

Molly leaned forward over the horse's neck just as she felt the needles of a pine branch brush her shoulder and back.

She quickly lost track of time, aware only that the riders moved slowly, first through a forest and then over rocky ground. Iron horseshoes clanged on stone. That sound and the rattle of gear and squeak of saddle leather were all that she heard. The men themselves were silent.

Uphill they rode and then down a steep slope; Molly felt coolness on her back as they moved into shade. Reaching bottom, her horse halted. She heard the two men dismount.

"All right," one of them said, "pull that sack off your head."

Molly reached up and lifted the flour sack. Bright light made her blink as she took the sack off, and she saw a white cloud of flour drift over her.

One of the masked men laughed suddenly. "God, lady, you look like a scary ghost."

"Put that gun away, mister," Molly said, throwing the sack down, "and I'll give you something to be scared of."

"Tough talk coming from a woman," he said, laughing.

"How tough are you without that gun?" she asked.

"Get on with it," the other man snapped.

Molly glanced around and saw that they had ridden into a low valley, shadowed from the afternoon sun. Unable to see the angle of the sun, she could not judge how much time had passed since she'd been run off the road. The distance from here to Cripple Creek might be four or five miles, ten or twelve, or more.

"Climb off that horse and get in there."

Molly looked over her shoulder as the first masked man motioned with his gun. He pointed to a small log cabin with a dirt roof. The plank door stood on shiny hinges, and hanging from the latch was a chain with a new padlock.

"Who put you men up to this?" she asked, realizing that her abduction had been planned.

"Get off that horse," the man repeated.

Molly made no move, and he came closer. "Lady, you can do this the easy way, or you can do it the hard way. I don't much like the idea of hurting a woman, but if that's what it takes to get this job done, then I'll do it."

Molly had thought of digging her heels into the horse and trying to escape but now decided against it. She heard a crude note of sincerity in the man's voice and had no doubt that he would shoot her down if he thought he had no other choice.

Leaning forward, Molly swung her leg over the horse's bare back. Her dress rode up as she slid to the ground.

"I'll be damned!" exclaimed the second masked man. "She's wearing a sneak gun!"

Molly realized too late that she had failed to keep her right leg covered and had revealed the holstered derringer.

"Gimme that damned thing," the first man ordered, cocking his revolver. "Go on, pull up your dress and hand it over."

Molly lifted her dress to her knees. She took the double-barreled derringer out of the holster strapped to her leg and held it out. The man snatched it away from her.

"Right purty legs," the other man said. "Maybe we ought to have a better look."

"Ain't got time for that," the first masked man snapped. He added, "Not now." He waved the revolver toward the cabin.

Molly turned and walked through the grass to the cabin door. When she reached it and stopped, she felt the prod of a gun barrel in her back. She pushed the door open and went inside.

The windowless cabin was no more than a log box ten or twelve feet square. By the light streaming through the doorway she saw a crate on the floor, a stack of blankets, and a chamber pot. In the crate were tins of food and a water jar.

One of the masked men brought a lantern in. He lifted the glass chimney and touched a match to the wick, adjusted it, then set the lantern down and backed out. The second man closed the door. Outside, Molly heard the chain rattle, then a *click* as the padlock was snapped shut.

She went to the door and quickly examined all four sides. It was secure, having been recently repaired. Whoever was behind her abduction had planned this operation carefully.

But who? The question echoed in her mind as she searched for an answer. Was it someone who knew she was the go-between with Winfield Shaw and Riley Newcomb? Someone who wanted to stop her from bringing the two sides together?

The first name that came to mind was Clint Lange. He was angrier than she'd ever seen him, and he was dead set against anyone who might aid Riley Newcomb's cause.

But as Molly looked around the cabin, she could not believe Clint had planned this. Someone else must have, perhaps one of the mine owners, or even a radical in the union movement who wanted to prevent Newcomb from forming a pact with Shaw.

Molly picked up the lantern and carried it around the cabin as she examined all the walls from top to bottom. She found the cabin to be solid, and fresh chinking between the logs prevented her from seeing outside.

She had managed to keep her handbag with her, but now did not feel so smart for having left her revolver behind. None of her tools would help her escape. The lock probes were useless because she could not get to the padlock outside.

Molly's gaze fell to the lantern in her hand, and she briefly considered setting fire to the door. But she decided against it. This little cabin was tight, and with no place for smoke to go, she'd be overcome long before flames could burn the door down.

She went to the door and pressed her ear to the slim gap between the edge of the door and the jamb. She listened intently but heard nothing, no stamp of a hoof or voices of the men.

Her abductors were either gone or had moved far enough away from the cabin that she could not hear them. She returned to the middle of the room and set the lantern on the floor. Kneeling on the blankets, she searched through the box, finding tins of food, an opener, a box of crackers, and one spoon.

For a moment, she wondered if she could dig her way out of here. The floor was dirt. But it was hard-packed dirt, and as she scratched at it and bent the spoon, she knew that idea was hopeless.

Discouraged, Molly spread the blanket out and lay down, using her handbag for a pillow. She closed her eyes, thinking she would not sleep but knowing that she needed rest.

Awakening with a start, she at first thought only a moment had passed. The lantern wick was low, and she slowly realized that she had slept and had been awakened by sounds outside.

Molly sat up when the chain on the door rattled. The door eased open, and in the widening gap was darkness. Night had fallen.

She edged back as a tall man wearing a bowler hat stepped into the pale light cast by the lantern. He was Leroy Luckett.

CHAPTER XX

Luckett stood over Molly, arms folded across his chest. Where his coat parted, she saw the walnut grips of a revolver sticking out of his waistband.

"I told you nobody plays me for a fool," he said.

"You were a fool to do this," Molly said, looking up at him. "Let me out of here."

Luckett laughed dryly. "I knew something about you didn't add up. Had a man keep track of you. You kept regular company with Clint Lange and Winfield Shaw, and you drove Pearl's buggy out to Newcomb's headquarters. So last night I wasn't one bit surprised to hear that Shaw was threatening to start negotiations with that union bastard. He was using you to get things going, wasn't he?"

Molly met his gaze but did not answer.

"So I got to thinking," Luckett said, "and wondered why you showed up in Cripple

Creek in the first place. And I figured it out. I sure did. Shaw used you to bribe Candace and get her out of town. Isn't that right?"

"Did she tell you that before you beat her to death?" Molly asked.

"You stinking bitch," Luckett said.

"Why did you kill her?" Molly asked. "Because she was leaving you? Because you'd lose a chance to pry $100,000 out of Winfield Shaw?"

Luckett closed the cabin door with his foot and shouldered out of his coat. "I'll show you what happens to any bitch who crosses me."

Molly scrambled to her feet and backed away from the slowly advancing Luckett. She saw his mouth curve into a grin. He was excited by pursuit, and she knew what he intended to do.

She bumped against the log wall, and Luckett moved swiftly toward her. She feinted in one direction and dodged the opposite way, avoiding his outstretched hand.

Luckett nearly lost his balance as he lunged, and when he wheeled around to face her, his face showed anger.

"Don't do this," Molly said, backing away.

"I have to teach you," Luckett said in a voice barely louder than a whisper. "Women don't learn unless I teach them —"

"Like you taught Candace?" Molly asked, backing toward a corner of the cabin.

Luckett smiled. He held his arms out at full length like an advancing bear.

"You grabbed her by the hair," Molly said, "and slammed her head against the bedstead, didn't you?"

Luckett bellowed and lunged for her.

Molly tried to dodge away but was caught in the corner and had little room. She felt his hard grip. His fingers sank into her arm.

She tried to turn and pull away but was lifted off her feet as Luckett encircled her waist with his other arm and picked her up. He dropped to one knee and threw her down on the dirt floor.

Molly felt her breath rush out of her lungs. She gasped, and Luckett came down on top of her. She struggled under his weight but could not move.

"I told you I get what I want," he said, sliding his hand to her waist. He pulled her dress up.

The moment Luckett shifted his weight, Molly brought one knee up, fast and hard.

Luckett moaned as he was banged squarely in the testicles. He rolled away, a pained expression in his eyes, swallowing hard.

Molly raised up, but before she could scramble away, Luckett's fist lashed out.

No time to duck the blow, Molly half turned. The punch caught her in the side below the ribs. She rolled away, bumping against the log wall. Dull pain throbbed through her body with every breath. She managed to sit and saw Luckett coming for her again, crawling on all fours.

Just as he reached her, Molly brought her right elbow up in a swift motion, striking his jaw. Luckett groaned and fell against her.

Molly quickly moved behind him, planted a knee in the small of his back, and grasped one of his wrists in both hands. She turned the wrist inward and drove his arm up his back between his shoulder blades.

Luckett moaned, then howled in pain.

"You're bust . . . busting . . . my arm!"

"I will break your arm," Molly said, leaning down over him, "if you don't tell me about Candace. You beat her to death, didn't you?"

Luckett groaned but did not answer.

Molly exerted more pressure on his arm, shoving it farther up on his back.

Luckett howled again but still did not reply.

Molly heard a horse whinny. Moments later came a voice she recognized as belonging to one of the masked riders who had brought her here.

"Lucky?" After a long pause, the man repeated, "Lucky? You in there?"

Molly said, "Get rid of him."

Luckett turned his head toward the door. He yelled, "She's got me —"

Molly quickly released him and rolled him over. She snatched the revolver out of his waistband and moved to the lantern on the floor near the food box. Grabbing up her handbag, she blew out the light.

Molly crawled to the door and thrust it open. In the starlight outside, she saw a man on horseback a dozen yards away. She raised the revolver and snapped off two quick shots, the bullets striking the ground near the horse. The animal reared.

When the horse came down, the rider turned him and rode away at a gallop. Molly fired twice more, intentionally wide, to keep him moving.

She got to her feet and stepped outside. Molly ran to the saddle horse Luckett had tied to a corner of the log cabin. Looping her handbag over the saddle horn, she untied the reins and swung up into the saddle. The horse skittered and threw his head, but she brought him under control and turned him, urging him away from the cabin.

By the faint light of stars, Molly found her way up the sloping side of the valley the way her abductors had brought her here, but beyond that general direction she did not have her bearings. Topping the ridge, she looked out into darkness and realized she could wander for most of the night without finding her way back to Cripple Creek.

Still she had little choice. The rider she'd run off would return with help, so she could not afford to stay at the cabin and question Luckett further. She briefly considered taking Luckett with her and turning him over to Marshal Broyles but saw that was too dangerous. Her only hope was to escape.

Riding along the ridge overlooking the shallow valley, Molly looked in the opposite direction. She saw the vague outline of a huge pine forest, distant hills, and miles beyond a mountainous horizon cut a jagged line in the night sky.

Molly reined up and dismounted. Whether she was able to find her way or not, she had a long ride in front of her, and Luckett's stirrups were too long.

She wrapped the reins around her wrist while she shortened the left stirrup, then the right one.

Coming around the horse, she saw a wink

of light in the distance. She stopped and stared, then led the horse down slope a few yards. Through a distant gap in the trees, several lights were visible.

They were not the lights of Cripple Creek, but they were too numerous to be only a cabin or even a cluster of cabins. They must mark a mine where a night shift was at work.

CHAPTER XXI

Molly found that the gold mine was surrounded by armed guards. A pair of them challenged her and warned her not to ride closer.

After she explained that she was lost, one of the guards gave her directions to the Cripple Creek road. Molly followed wagonwheel ruts leading away from the mine through the trees, and by starlight she found the main road.

Molly arrived in town long after midnight. Myers Avenue was quiet, and most of the windows in the buildings lining the street were dark. She tied the saddle horse at the hitching post in front of the Old Homestead and used her key to enter through the back door. A gas lamp lighted the hallway.

"Molly!" Pearl exclaimed, rushing out of the front parlor to her. "Where on earth have you been?" The big woman wore flowing nightclothes, and she grasped Molly by the arms.

Molly nearly collapsed against her. Pearl led her into her room. She slumped down on the bed, drank a glass of water that Pearl brought, and described her abduction and all that happened afterward.

"Lucky?" Pearl said in a tone of disbelief. "I can't imagine he'd do such a thing."

"He did," Molly said, "and in the morning I'm going to have a talk with Marshal Broyles. But right now I need to report to Mr. Shaw."

Pearl reacted strongly to that. "Molly, you're in no shape to go anywhere. You can hardly stand." She brushed a hand through her hair. "And if you don't mind my saying so, you look a fright. What's this white stuff caked in your hair?"

Molly realized Pearl was right. She explained how she had become dusted with flour, then asked, "Can you have someone deliver a written message to Mr. Shaw? It's important."

"Yes, of course," Pearl said. "I'll bring you some paper." She left the room and presently came back with a pen and ink well and several sheets of stationery.

Molly wrote a brief account of what had happened to her, explaining to Shaw why she had failed to complete her mission. She offered to see Newcomb in the morning and now awaited instructions.

Molly ate a late breakfast of scrambled eggs and ham and muffins freshly baked by Colleen. Afterward, she took a hot bath. Even though she was sore muscled and bruised where Luckett had punched her, Molly came out of the tub feeling refreshed. As soon as she dressed, she asked Pearl to send for Marshal Broyles.

Molly met the big lawman in the front parlor of the Old Homestead. The room was empty at this early hour and smelled vaguely of stale cigar smoke. Broyles sat on one of the upholstered settees, long legs stretched out in front of him, and soberly listened to Molly's account of her abduction. His sad, bulldog expression changed little until he heard Luckett's name.

"Now let me see if I got this straight," Broyles said, leaning forward to prop his elbows on his knees. "Two masked men locked you in some cabin, and the next thing you know, the door opens and Lucky walks in. And he assaults you."

Molly nodded. "He tried to."

"Did he *hurt* you?" Broyles asked.

"Not in the way you mean," Molly said.

"I defended myself and got away from him." She went on to describe her escape in the night and how she found her way back to Cripple Creek.

"Where was this cabin?" Broyles asked.

"I don't know," Molly said. "I'd estimate it's six or seven miles away and off the Cripple Creek road another two or three miles. Maybe more."

"What direction?" he asked.

"I can't say exactly," Molly said. "I was run off the left side of the road, so I guess we started out in a westerly direction. But where we went from there, I don't know."

Broyles studied her. "Well, what was the name of the mine where you got directions back to town?"

"I don't know that, either," Molly said. "The guards wouldn't let me get close to the buildings."

A long silence followed. Broyles dragged a hand across his jaw. "Well, Miss Owens, I'll look into this. First thing, I'll see if I can locate Pearl's buggy and then I'll go have a talk with Lucky."

The lawman stood and put on his cap. Molly followed him out of the parlor to the front door, aware that he was skeptical of her account. She had to admit that she'd been unable to provide any solid evidence to back up her story.

As Broyles reached the door, Molly said, "What I told you is true, marshal — every word."

He turned to her and touched his hand to his cap. "Yes, ma'am," he said, and turned and opened the door. As he walked away, Molly saw that Luckett's horse was no longer tied at the post.

An hour later, Winfield Shaw entered the Old Homestead through the back door. Molly showed him into her room and explained in more detail what had happened to her the previous day. Shaw nodded grimly as she spoke. He had no difficulty in believing Luckett was behind her abduction.

"The strikebreakers arrived on a private train last night," he said. "It makes sense that Lucky would want to put you away for a while. He probably had the blessing of some of the mine owners." He added, "We're going to have to do something about Mr. Luckett."

"I have done something about him," Molly said. She related her conversation with Broyles.

"Broyles is all right as town marshal," Shaw said, "but don't expect him to investigate much. He doesn't have the head for it."

Shaw went on. "I sent Clint to Denver with my personal request for troops. I want the governor to move quickly. With the strikebreakers in town, we're close to a war around here. A shot fired now could turn this district into a battle ground."

"You still want me to carry your message to Riley Newcomb?" Molly asked.

"Yes, I do," Shaw said. "This time, I'll send some men to ride with you — men with guns."

Molly shook her head. "I'd prefer to go alone. Those miners guarding Newcomb were jumpy twenty-four hours ago. By now they're probably trigger happy. If I rode in there with your men, they might shoot first and ask questions later." She added, "What I do need is a good saddle horse."

"I'll see that you get one," Shaw said, "right away."

"If I'd been on horseback yesterday," Molly said, "and carrying my revolver in my shoulder holster, things would have come out differently."

Shaw regarded her for a moment. "You know, Miss Owens, a man could be fooled by your good looks and that sweet, innocent face of yours. You've got steel in your back-bone."

Half an hour after Winfield Shaw left the

Old Homestead, a rangy, deep-chested gelding was delivered to the rear entrance of the brothel. Molly went out and quickly examined the horse. He was buckskin in color, and she judged the animal to be strong rather than fast, typical of mountain horses.

She changed to her riding skirt and wore a light jacket over her blouse. Under the jacket, in a cutaway holster that fit snugly under her arm, was her Colt Lightning Model .38.

As she rode along the now-familiar road leading out of Cripple Creek, Molly kept an eye out for riders who might be following. Ahead, she scanned the tree line on either side of the rutted road, watching for concealed horsemen. She saw none. The only traffic was made up of ore wagons.

Several loaded ore wagons passed by, heading for the railroad. Molly noticed that the teamsters now shared their wagon seats with men armed with pistols in their belts and rifles or shotguns propped on their knees.

The buckskin gelding, she discovered, was a fine saddle horse. The animal possessed a long and smooth gait that covered distance with remarkable speed. Plenty of horses could outrun this one in an eighth or quarter of a mile, but for a long run she would bet on this sturdy horse, particularly at high altitudes.

Molly turned off the road and topped the hill overlooking Riley Newcomb's cabin. In the grassy valley down there, she saw several buckboards and flat-bed wagons around one of the slab outbuildings. In the shade of that structure, saddle horses and mules were tied around a water trough.

Riding down the slope, Molly heard a shout. By the time she reached the yard in front of the cabin, a group of miners streamed out of the outbuilding, all carrying guns.

"That's close enough, lady," one of the men said, waving a rusty double-barreled shotgun at her. "Whaddya want?"

"I'm here to see Riley Newcomb," Molly said, looking for the miners who had confronted her the last time she had come here. But among the upturned faces she saw none that were familiar. She added, "He's expecting me."

"The hell you say," the miner said. He was a stout, deep-voiced man, wearing overalls and boots, a dark wool shirt, and a wide-brimmed felt hat on his head.

Another miner came a step closer. He carried a small-caliber rifle in the crook of his arm. "Riley ain't expecting you." He staggered, clearly drunk.

"Ask him," Molly said, realizing all the men had been drinking.

A third man said, "Climb off that big hoss, lady, so's we can search you. Riley says to search anyone who comes along."

Several men guffawed, and as Molly was considering whether she should turn the gelding and ride out, another miner came forward and grasped the reins under the bit. A fourth man moved swiftly to her side and reached up, grasping her around the waist. He yanked her out of the saddle.

Molly landed on her feet, raised her arm, and snapped her elbow back into the miner's face. He released her and fell to his knees, gingerly cupping his hands around his nose. Tears streamed from his eyes.

"Gentlemen," Molly said, "I don't like to be manhandled."

The group of miners stared at her in shocked silence, unable to believe that this woman had dropped a big man with a single blow.

"What the hell's going on here?"

The miners parted sheepishly as Riley Newcomb came through the group. His eyes widened when he saw Molly. Then he glanced at the miner on his knees. Still holding his hands to his face, the man rocked back and forth, moaning.

"Looks like you men got more than you bargained for," Newcomb said.

The miner carrying the rusty shotgun said, "Hell, Riley, she claimed you was expecting her."

"I am," Newcomb said. He turned to Molly. "I'm glad you're here, and I apologize if these men have been rude or abusive to you."

Molly smiled. "Now that we've come to an understanding, no apologies are necessary." She looked at each man, then turned and walked with Newcomb to the cabin.

CHAPTER XXII

"Shaw is twenty-four hours too late," Riley Newcomb said after Molly told him the millionaire had agreed to raise wages to $3.50 at the Independence and all of his other mining properties.

Newcomb went on. "My information was correct. The damned mine owners have brought in thugs, and we're preparing to defend ourselves."

Molly told him of her abduction to explain why Winfield Shaw's message had been delayed.

"Luckett is a low-grade bastard," Newcomb said. "I'm amazed that you're still working for the mine owners."

"I'm working for Winfield Shaw," Molly said. "He wants nothing to do with Luckett or with strikebreakers. To prevent bloodshed, he's sent Clint Lange to Denver with a request for the state militia. Troops may be on their way right now."

"I'll believe that when I see the color of their uniforms," Newcomb said.

Molly felt exasperated by the man's deep suspicion of Shaw. "It's true," she said softly.

"Well, those troops had better get here in a hurry," Newcomb said.

"What's going to happen?" Molly asked.

Newcomb did not answer for a long moment. "Let's just say that the miners will keep the mines shut down until the owners give up that half dollar."

"You mean, you expect a battle at every mine site challenged by the strikebreakers," Molly said.

Newcomb replied with a single nod of his head.

"But can't you avoid a conflict by announcing your settlement with Shaw?" Molly said. "You've said yourself that the other mines will follow the lead of the Independence."

"That was before strikebreakers were hired," Newcomb said. "Now we have to either stand up or see the union busted. The best thing Shaw can do is to convince the other mine owners to raise wages."

Molly rode back to Cripple Creek, fully realizing that an opportunity to make peace had been lost. Events were moving swiftly now, and she had the powerless, dreamlike sensation that she was watching a collision between two powerful forces.

In town, she rode down Myers Avenue to the Old Homestead. On the flower-lined walk there, she saw Marshal Broyles. He had evidently just come out, and when he looked up and saw her, he stopped.

"I'd like to have a word with you, Miss Owens," Broyles said.

Molly reined up and dismounted, tying the reins of the big buckskin to the hitching post. "Let's go inside," she said, thinking now she could press charges against Luckett and at least have that as one small victory in what appeared to be a losing cause.

In the front parlor of the Old Homestead, Broyles declined the chair Molly offered and stood in the middle of the room holding his cap in both hands before him.

"I found Pearl's buggy just where you said it would be," he said, "and her horse was seen grazing outside of town a ways." He paused.

"I talked to Lucky," Broyles went on, speaking in a deliberate tone of voice, "and, well, he's stove up. Got his arm in a sling and hasn't been able to do much for the last twenty-four hours. Says he hasn't left Cripple Creek —"

"He's lying," Molly said. "His arm is in a sling because I bent it behind his back last night."

Broyles stared at her. "Now, Miss Owens, Lucky is a pretty fair-sized man —"

"What you're saying is," Molly said, "that you believe his story, not mine."

"I don't have any proof that what you told me is true," he said. "In fact, Lucky claims you've lied about him before. Says you accused him of having something to do with the death of Candace Smith. Is that true?"

Molly nodded.

"Got any evidence of that?" he asked.

"No," she admitted. "Not any that I could bring into a court of law."

Broyles reached into his coat pocket and brought out an empty laudanum vial. "I found this on the floor boards of Pearl's buggy."

Molly exhaled. "I should have seen this coming."

"Is it yours?" he asked.

"No," Molly said.

Broyles studied her. "Maybe you had a runaway yesterday and you don't remember everything that happened."

"I don't use that drug, marshal," she said, "or any other."

"Well, now, Miss Owens," he said, "you

understand that I have to go on the evidence that I find during an investigation, and I just haven't seen any that favors your account of what happened to you yesterday."

Molly exhaled and folded her arms across her chest. "Now there's one other thing," Broyles said. "As an officer of the law, I'm ordering you not to harass Leroy Luckett and not to spread stories about him having something to do with the death of Candace Smith."

"Sure," Molly said, "I'll quit picking on him."

"You'd better take this matter seriously," Broyles said, "or I'll come looking for you if I hear that you've been spreading stories that are damaging to Lucky's character and standing in the community."

Molly looked into the man's bulldog face, realizing that he used that tone of voice for newcomers who weren't welcome, that no matter what anyone else thought of Leroy Luckett, the marshal would take his side in a dispute.

Soon after Broyles left the Old Homestead, Molly went out to her horse, swung up into the saddle, and rode out of Cripple Creek. This time, she left town in the opposite direction, following the steep and narrow ore-wagon road that wound up the side of Gold Hill toward the Independence and other prosperous mines. She found Winfield Shaw in his cabin eating a meal of fresh oyster soup and crackers.

Shaw abruptly pushed the bowl away — a soup bowl of Haviland china, Molly noticed — and listened intently while she described her meeting with Riley Newcomb.

"He lumps me in with all the other mine owners," Shaw said after Molly finished, "and he doesn't trust any of us."

Molly nodded. "His back is against the wall, and he's ready for a fight."

"So are the strikebreakers," Shaw said. "They've been armed with .45-caliber revolvers and repeating rifles." He paused, and as he exhaled, a tired expression came over his dour face, making him look much older than he was.

"I'm the man who made the first gold discovery in this district," Shaw went on. "Up until that time, all I'd ever thought about was making my fortune. That dream was what kept me living and breathing. Well, I made my fortune, more than I ever dreamed of. It's brought me some joy and plenty of grief. Now if it brings violence and death, that'll be the final price, a price extracted from me."

"What do you mean?" Molly asked when he fell silent.

Shaw was either too deep in his thoughts to hear, or he chose not to reply. "You know, a miner deserves to earn as much money as a carpenter or any other craftsman, but no one deserves to die for it."

Shaw blinked and turned to Molly. "I'm worried about Clint. Haven't heard from him since he wired a message that the governor had agreed to send troops down here."

"Maybe he's on his way with a trainload of militiamen," Molly said.

"Maybe." He thought a moment. "Miss Owens, you know who stands to profit the most from this whole mess?"

Molly nodded. "Leroy Luckett."

"That's right," Shaw said. "The man has a knack for prospering off the misery of others. Lucky was well paid to bring in the strikebreakers, and now he's being paid to house and feed them. Every day they're here, he's making money. I wish there was a way to put that leech out of business."

"So do I," Molly said. "So do I."

CHAPTER XXIII

In the evening, Molly was taken aside by Pearl to a corner of the Old Homestead's front parlor.

In a whisper, Pearl explained that she had just learned from a talkative "guest" that the strikebreakers, thirty men strong, were being lodged in a boarding house on the far end of Third Street. The boarding house was one of many in Cripple Creek that had recently been vacated by miners who were out of work and unable to pay rent.

"The talk I hear," Pearl went on, "is that this strike will be busted in a day or two. The strikebreakers are hard men, ready for business."

"So are the miners," Molly said.

Two hours after midnight, she was still unable to sleep. For the last hour, she had lain in bed while the music and raucous voices from saloons and dance halls down the street softened and declined to silence.

Feeling restless, she got out of bed. She had an idea, a good one, that she could not put out of her mind.

Myers Avenue was empty when Molly hastily crossed the street, and she slipped into the dark shadow between two buildings confident that she had not been seen. The passageway was as black as ink. Slowly placing one foot in front of the other, she moved through the passageway to the back alley.

Standing at the corners of the two frame buildings for several minutes, Molly peered into the night. By the faint light of stars, she watched for movement in the alley, for the cautious figure of a night deputy or a staggering drunk, but she saw no one.

Molly stepped into the alley and followed it to the rear of the Gold Coin Club. The building was dark. She moved to the windowless door and heard a shrill creak of wood as she stepped up on the stoop. Molly turned and looked at the other darkened buildings. No lights flared behind the black windows.

She turned and grasped the cold door handle, turned it, and felt the latch stop against the lock. Bending down, she touched the keyhole with her fingertips. The lock was a common type, requiring a skeleton key to release it.

Molly drew out a ring of master skeleton keys from her handbag. She inserted the largest one into the keyhole, discovering that it was too thick. She slid her fingers down the ring to the smaller keys. The fourth one she tried in the lock opened the door.

Molly walked into the back hallway after locking the door behind her. The darkness smelled of stale pipe and cigar smoke and whiskey. She stood still for several minutes, listening. Hearing no sounds, she moved slowly down the hall. Her fingers touched the wall until she felt the door to Luckett's office. She found the lock under the door handle and opened it with the same skeleton key.

Molly stepped into the office and closed the door. In the pitch-dark room, she fumbled for a match in her handbag, drew one out, and struck it. The match head sputtered and flared and cast dancing shadows on the office walls.

She looked around at the furnishings, the roll-top desk, the safe in the corner of the office, Persian carpet on the floor, and the high-backed leather upholstered chairs around a low table holding a decanter of bourbon.

Molly moved to the desk, reaching for a lamp there. She lifted the glass chimney and touched the flame to the blackened wick. The light brightened the room as she replaced the chimney.

She sat in Luckett's swivel chair and opened all the drawers in the roll-top desk. She didn't know what she was looking for, but she methodically went through all the papers she found, reading and scanning the contents. Most were of a kind she'd expect to find in a club owner's files — order forms from breweries and liquor distributors and forms for other supplies such as cigars and plug tobacco. In a bottom drawer, she discovered letters, and these she read more carefully.

Many were from a brewery owner in Colorado Springs. Luckett evidently had a dispute with him over some outstanding orders. The tone of the letters was apologetic, polite phrases of a businessman who did not want to lose a customer.

In the bottom of the drawer were letters written by women. All concerned employment, and as Molly read through them and saw references to red-light districts in Aspen, Leadville, and Denver, she realized these were written by prostitutes who wanted to work in Myers Avenue cribs owned by Luckett. One scrawled note bore the signature of Candace Smith.

The letters were remarkably similar and struck Molly as being uniformly sad. Women who made these applications were like Candace and the fat woman in the crib next door. Unwanted in sporting houses, they believed that a crib on the edge of town was all that was left to them. At least in booming Cripple Creek they had a hope of making a living.

Molly returned the letters to the drawer, put the brewery correspondence on top of them, and closed the drawer. Turning in the swivel chair, her eyes went to the safe.

Last time she was here, she'd recognized it as one manufactured by the Stone & Barnes Company of Chicago. Molly's Fenton training in safecracking had come from an old, garrulous ex-convict who termed the Stone & Barnes steel boxes "pie safes" because they were "as easy as pie" to open.

From this old man, she'd learned to listen for the tumblers as she slowly turned the dial. A combination of three fell into place, and after hearing them click in order, she turned the dial to the right, back left two full turns, then right again one turn or less, listening to the tumblers.

Molly missed the combination the first time, but the second time around the sequence, she got it. She pulled the handle down, and the safe door swung open.

By lamplight, she examined the contents of the safe. On shelves she found several property deeds, shares of stock in various mines, ore samples ranging in size from a thimble to a melon, and cash. By quick estimate, she determined the amount to be about $18,000. Behind the stacks of greenbacks and gold coins, she discovered a small envelope, unsealed.

Molly lifted the envelope out and opened the flap. Holding it toward the lamp she saw several gold rings inside and the glitter of a tiny diamond.

She shook the diamond ring out of the envelope into the palm of her hand. She knew immediately that she'd last seen this ring on Candace Smith's hand.

A wave of anger swept over Molly. She sat on the carpeted floor of Luckett's office, debating whether or not to take this ring with her. She took a deep breath, then dropped the ring back into the envelope and returned it to the safe. She closed the heavy door and latched it. The ring was evidence that removed all doubt from her mind about Luckett's guilt, but it was not final proof that he had murdered Candace. Leaving the ring here left intact a growing chain of evidence against the man.

Sudden rattling of the back door jarred Molly out of her thoughts. She scrambled to her feet, snatched up her handbag, and blew out the lamp.

In the darkness, Molly drew her revolver out of her shoulder holster and moved to the office door. She heard no sounds. She opened the door and edged out into the hall. It was empty.

She closed the door and locked it and walked down the hall to the back door. After unlocking it with her skeleton key, she eased the door open and stepped outside. Just as she shut the door, she glimpsed movement in the alley.

By starlight, she saw a glint of brass buttons on a deputy. He was on night patrol, now checking the building next door. He checked each window and gave the back door there a vigorous shake.

Molly pressed against the door, watching the lawman move on. When he was out of sight, she locked the door and moved away, hurrying down the alley the way she'd come.

Early in the morning, Winfield Shaw

came to the Old Homestead for breakfast. Molly met him in the dining room where he had taken a chair at the table beside Pearl. Colleen came into the room with a pot of coffee and warm cinnamon rolls on a tray.

After the Irish girl left, Shaw said, "Clint wired a message to me a couple of hours ago. He was on his way down here with a carload of troops, but the train derailed a few miles out of Denver."

"Oh, no!" Pearl whispered.

"Is Clint all right?" Molly asked.

Shaw nodded. "He's all right, but some of the men were hurt. They've returned to Denver." He paused. "My plan is shot to hell. All I can do now is buy some time and hope the troops can get here tonight or tomorrow morning."

"Buy time?" Molly asked. The thought crossed her mind that the one thing Shaw's millions could not buy, or even influence, was time.

"I want to meet publicly with Newcomb," Shaw said. "In full view of everyone, I'll sign his contract. Maybe that'll cool things down."

He looked at Molly. "The strikebreakers are ready to move. I hear they'll start with the American Eagle Mine, just over the ridge from my Independence. They plan to run the striking miners out of there and bring in a new crew. Before that happens, I want to meet with Newcomb."

"And you want me to set it up?" Molly asked.

"That's right," Shaw said. He added emphatically, "But I don't want you to do anything that will endanger your life. If things look bad, turn around and come back."

Molly sipped coffee and hurriedly ate a cinnamon roll. "Can you have that big buckskin horse sent over?" she asked, standing.

A brief smile came to Shaw's face as he looked up at her. "I already have."

CHAPTER XXIV

The big gelding pranced and danced sideways down Myers Avenue. Molly held a tight rein on the horse's powerful friskiness, but when she reached the end of the street and turned on to the road out of Cripple Creek, she gave the buckskin his head. With nothing but open road ahead, the horse lunged away, breaking into a long-legged gallop.

Molly soon discovered that she was too late, and no amount of running would change it. As she topped the hill overlooking the cabin, the bitter scent of smoke came to her nostrils.

The log cabin still smoldered. She slowly rode down the grassy hill toward it, seeing the dirt roof caved in on one side, the small windows broken out, and the blackened plank door off its hinges. The largest outbuilding was burned down, and the ground near the trough there was littered with half a dozen dead saddle horses and mules.

As Molly circled the smoldering wreckage, she saw that the animals had been shot. The scorched logs of the cabin were pockmarked with bullet holes, too. A battle had raged here, probably at dawn. News of it had yet to travel to Cripple Creek. Molly rode away at a trot, wondering if Riley Newcomb had survived.

Remembering Winfield Shaw's remark that the American Eagle Mine was "just over the ridge" from the Independence, Molly headed back for Cripple Creek. Skirting the town, she followed the bank of a stream to the base of Gold Hill and angled up the slope in a direction she judged would bring her to the top a hundred yards or so beyond Shaw's property.

On the way up slope, she guided the horse through a stand of spruce trees. The air was ripe with forest smells, mingling odors of growth and decay.

The horse spooked four deer bedded down among the trees. They were does, one with a fawn, and Molly watched them spring up and bound away, their small, pointed hoofs silently striking the earth. Farther up, a Steller's Jay loudly called from a tree top, letting Molly know that she was trespassing and unwelcome. The bird, blue as the sky over Cripple Creek, did not fall silent until Molly was long past.

She found the top of Gold Hill to be open ground, covered by short grass sprinkled with white and yellow wildflowers, no bigger in size than buttons. At the crest of the hill, she reined up and dismounted.

Tying the horse's reins to a shrub, she walked down the far slope fifty yards. Tin roofs of mine buildings came into view to her right, and as she walked downhill in that direction, she saw the top of a head frame. A sign in gold letters on the crosspiece of the head frame read AMERICAN EAGLE MINE.

Another dozen paces downhill and Molly ducked down. Amid piles of rock and soil beyond the mine buildings were crouching men. They were miners, armed with rifles or shotguns. They seemed intent on something beyond the mine dump, something concealed from Molly's view in a stand of aspen trees.

Molly slowly crawled to one side, and she saw an ore-wagon road in the trees. A dead horse was there, and in the shadows of the white-barked trees were men. They must have arrived on that road and were confronted by the miners.

A shot was fired, and Molly slid down behind a rock. From there she overlooked the American Eagle Mine, seeing the crouching miners on her left, and in the trees to her right were the strikebreakers. They were probably now planning their attack.

The miners were few in number — eight by Molly's count. Riley Newcomb was not among them.

In the next instant, shots were fired from the trees. Thirty men in the grove must have emptied their repeating rifles, laying down withering fire that slammed into the mine dump and buildings beyond. Ricocheting bullets sang through the air, and Molly glimpsed the miners hugging the ground the second before she lay flat on the sloping hillside behind the rock that protected her.

When the firing stopped abruptly, Molly looked up and saw men dashing through the trees. She suddenly realized the strikebreakers were dispersing, and would try to outflank the trapped miners.

Several men dashed out of the trees with drawn hand guns. They were led by Leroy Luckett.

Molly wanted to cry out, to somehow warn those eight men that they were about to be slaughtered, when a single shot came from the hillside directly below her. Someone was hiding down there, just out of her view, and obviously the miners had been waiting for his signal. They quickly fell back. One of the men paused, and when he ran to join the others dashing away from the mine buildings, Molly saw that he left behind a smoking fuse.

Molly heard a clatter of stones, and in the next moment a man came running up the hillside directly toward her. He was Riley Newcomb.

Newcomb's eyes widened when he looked up and saw her. He frantically waved. "Get out of here!"

Molly scrambled to her feet. Newcomb reached her, and together they sprinted up to the top of the hill. Newcomb pulled her to the ground just as they reached it, and from behind came a tremendous explosion. A deafening shudder followed, and Molly clasped her hands over her ears.

She rolled over and looked back. A cloud of smoke and dust billowed into the air, and tumbling to the ground were boards and tin roofs, torn and bent like lids cut out of cans.

Her ears ringing, she barely heard Newcomb's question: "What're you doing here?"

"Looking . . . for you," she said.

He glanced around. "We have to get out of here."

Molly thought quickly. "We can ride

double on my horse."

"This wasn't in my plan —" he began.

"Come on," Molly interrupted. She scrambled to her feet and ran, glancing over her shoulder to see Newcomb following.

The gelding pranced, pulling the reins taut. Molly realized that if she had not tied him securely, the animal would have run straight back to Cripple Creek.

Riding double, Molly headed over the hill toward the Independence Mine. When the road came into sight, she saw a wagon. Half a dozen miners were in the wagon bed, evidently a rescue party from the Independence on their way to the American Eagle. They probably believed a mining accident had happened there.

After the wagon was gone, Molly guided the horse down through the forest, joined the road, and followed it to Winfield Shaw's cabin.

"What the hell are you doing?" Newcomb whispered.

"You need to disappear for a while, don't you?" she asked. "This is the one place in the whole district where you'll be safe."

She reined up at the cabin door. An armed guard came out. Molly recognized him as the man who had driven Shaw's buggy for her.

"We're here to see Mr. Shaw," Molly said.

The guard looked at her, then at Newcomb. "He's in town, meeting the train."

For a moment, Molly considered going to the depot herself. Perhaps Clint and the state militia were there. But she quickly discarded the idea. "Will he come back here?"

"I reckon so," the guard said. "That big explosion, whatever it was, will bring him running."

"We'll wait for him," Molly said. Seeing a troubled expression on the guard's face, she asked, "It's all right, isn't it?"

"Yeah," the guard said. "Mr. Shaw says you get the red carpet around here — anything you want." He jerked his head at Newcomb. "I don't know that fellar, though."

"He's all right," Molly said. "Mr. Shaw wants to see him."

The guard nodded and took the horse's reins as Molly and Riley Newcomb dismounted.

"I feel like I'm walking into the lion's den," Newcomb said after the guard had taken the gelding to a lean-to behind the cabin.

Molly went to the cabin door and held it open for him. "Some lion's den."

Newcomb cast a questioning look at her until he entered Shaw's cabin. Then his mouth dropped open. A moment passed before he recovered, looked around at the splendor, and laughed aloud.

"I always thought millionaires were crazy," Newcomb said. "Now I know it for a fact."

"Mr. Shaw can afford some eccentricities," Molly said, but she saw Newcomb shake his head in disagreement as he brought his gaze back from the crystal chandelier.

"No," Newcomb said, "he's loco."

Less than an hour later, the front door swung open, and Winfield Shaw strode in, stopping short when he saw Riley Newcomb seated at his dining-room table. Behind Shaw came Clint, a look of anger settling over his face.

CHAPTER XXV

The three men were struck silent for a long moment as they stared at one another. Molly pushed her chair back and stood.

"I believe you gentlemen have met," she said.

Newcomb rose, warily watching them.

"Get out," Clint said.

From his tone, Molly realized he meant both she and Newcomb should leave.

Shaw raised a hand in front of Clint, then came forward, extending the same hand to Newcomb.

Riley Newcomb met him halfway and gave him a brief handshake. "Miss Owens tells me you wanted a meeting. Call your dog off and you'll have it."

Clint swore and came at Newcomb, fists clenched.

Molly quickly moved in front of Clint. "Come outside with me," she whispered.

"I'm not leaving Win alone with this murdering outlaw," he said loudly.

Molly leaned against him, physically blocking his way. She felt the tension in the man's stiff body, and she heard his deep breathing. Despite the danger of the moment, she remembered him as a lover.

"It's all right, Clint," Shaw said. "Wait outside."

Clint resisted when Molly took his arm. But after glaring at Newcomb for several seconds, he turned and walked swiftly to the door, leaving Molly behind.

She followed him outside, glanced back at Newcomb and Shaw, and closed the cabin door.

"If anything happens in there," Clint said menacingly, "you're responsible for it."

"I know," Molly said.

"I misjudged you," he said. "I thought you'd remember who you worked for, that you were loyal —"

"I am loyal," Molly interrupted, "to Winfield Shaw."

"You're loyal to Newcomb," he countered. "By bringing him here, you've done more to advance his cause than anyone else could have."

"While you were gone," she said, "Mr. Shaw sent me to Newcomb with a message. He wanted to arrange a meeting in a public place where a new contract would be signed."

"Hell, I know all about that scheme," Clint said angrily, "and I've told you Win is misguided. If he signs, the district will blow up."

"The district blew up about two hours ago, Clint," Molly said.

He nodded. "Win and I heard about the American Eagle. That's all the more reason you ought to be on my side. Newcomb is responsible for laying waste to one of the biggest mines in Cripple Creek. Men were injured there."

"The strikebreakers were the ones who attacked," Molly said. "The miners didn't start it."

"Sure," Clint said, "that's the story Newcomb wants people to believe."

"It's true," Molly said. "The strikebreakers would have slaughtered the miners if they'd had the chance. I know. I was there. I saw the whole thing."

Molly went on to explain what had happened that morning; then she described her abduction by Luckett.

"I'll be damned," Clint said. He paused. "Well, it doesn't change anything. Newcomb forced the issue by calling this strike. If he wins, the mine owners will lose control of their profits."

"They'll lose half a dollar a day per miner," Molly said. "Miners want to earn as much as other craftsmen."

"Now you do sound like Riley Newcomb," Clint said.

"Mr. Shaw was a carpenter," Molly said, "and he agrees with Newcomb."

Clint pursed his lips. "Win is blind to the larger issue at stake."

"Violence is the issue at stake right now," Molly said. "Did you bring the state militia?"

Clint shook his head. "Half a dozen troopers were injured in the derailment. One was the colonel in charge. Without him, no one was willing to take the lead. When I got back to Denver, I asked the governor to send a request for help to Washington."

"Will federal troops come here?" Molly asked.

"Either troops or U.S. marshals," Clint said. "I hope marshals will be sent. They can be on their way almost immediately once the order comes through."

Clint half turned away from her and folded his arms across his chest. His expression was grim.

"What's happened to us, Clint?" Molly asked.

He did not reply.

Molly left his side and walked back to the door of the cabin. A few minutes later, the door swung open. Riley Newcomb came out, followed by Shaw.

"Clint, I want you to draw up a contract with the union," Shaw said. "I've agreed to Mr. Newcomb's terms, and he's promised not to strike the Independence or any of my other properties. I want two copies of a document with those terms brought up here."

Shaw glanced at Molly. "I'm hoping that news of this agreement will cool some tempers, but in view of what happened this morning at the American Eagle, Mr. Newcomb and I have agreed that it is best not to make a public spectacle of the signing."

A long moment of silence followed, and Molly saw Clint staring at Shaw.

"Clint," Shaw said in a low voice, "I want that agreement within the hour."

For a time, Molly thought Clint would defy his employer, but then he nodded curtly and turned away, striding to his horse.

Sporadic fighting between miners and small groups of strikebreakers continued at various mines throughout the afternoon and early evening. News of gun battles filtered back to Myers Avenue all afternoon, and wounded men, stretched out in ore wagons, arrived at the Cripple Creek hospital.

Molly had witnessed the signing of the agreement between Winfield Shaw and Riley Newcomb; then she had left Gold Hill and returned to the Old Homestead.

News of the "Independence Agreement" swept through the Cripple Creek saloon district after dark and was met by triumphant cheers and the firing of revolvers into the night sky. But as far as Molly could tell, no tempers were cooled. The miners seemed more determined than ever to strike until the other big mines complied.

Before midnight came the awaited announcement from the three mine owners who had given the original order for an increase in shift hours with no raise in wages: they would not abide by the Independence Agreement.

This was met by renewed shouts by miners gathered on Myers Avenue as they threatened to shut down every mine in the district.

In the Old Homestead, Molly learned from Pearl that more strikebreakers would arrive by special train tomorrow. This had come from Red Rose, who in turn had heard it from a guest she'd plied with champagne. The man held a partnership with the owner of one of the struck mines. He claimed that once the strikebreakers were assembled, an all-out effort would be made to dislodge the miners from the El Paso and Jackpot mines.

Molly knew those were two of the big operations whose owners had originally posted notices of the nine-hour shifts.

In the morning, she rode her horse up the Gold Hill road to Shaw's cabin. As she turned off the road toward the log cabin, she saw the millionaire climbing into his buggy.

"Leave that horse here," Shaw said when he saw Molly riding into the yard, "and come with me."

Sitting in the buggy beside Shaw, Molly listened while he explained why he was in a hurry. He had just received a telegraphed message that federal marshals were arriving by train, and it was up to Shaw to meet them and arrange for food and housing. Right now, Clint was searching the hotels on Bennett Avenue for empty rooms.

At the depot, Molly stood on the loading platform with the millionaire as the train rolled in and stopped. Nine marshals climbed off a passenger coach behind the coal car. Molly spotted the men immediately. They were led by Joe Sears.

CHAPTER XXVI

"What're you doing here?" Sears demanded. He was a squat, round-shouldered man, built like a barrel with legs, with a wide face and a round nose perched above thick lips. A cartridge belt looped around his waist, and in the holster on his right hip was a Smith & Wesson .38 revolver.

Molly met his hostile stare, then said, "Marshal, this is Winfield Shaw." Turning to the millionaire, she said, "Mr. Shaw, this is Joe Sears, a federal marshal stationed in Denver."

Shaw thrust out his hand to shake. "Glad to meet you, marshal. How many men are in your force?"

Sears pulled his gaze away from Molly and shook Winfield Shaw's outstretched hand. "Just the nine of us."

In obvious disappointment, Shaw looked past him at the eight marshals standing on the railroad loading platform. Each man carried a grip in one hand and a repeating rifle in the other.

"You're outnumbered by the strike-breakers," Shaw observed, "and by the miners."

"We have powers of arrest," Sears said, "and I'll get the cooperation of the town marshal." He added, "If I have to arrest all the thugs in Cripple Creek and ship them to the state pen for custody, I'll do it."

Molly saw Shaw regard this stocky federal marshal. "That would be quite a task."

"Where will we be lodged, Mr. Shaw?" Sears asked.

"I have a man looking for hotel rooms right at this moment," he replied. He drew a gold watch from his vest pocket. "In a quarter of an hour, he's scheduled to report to me."

"All right," Sears said. "And you'll have horses for us?"

"I will," Shaw said.

"Then if you'll direct me to your town marshal's office," Sears said, "I'll wait for you there."

Winfield Shaw half turned, facing the sprawling town. "Straight down that street," he said, pointing to Bennett Avenue. "Beyond the divided section of street there, go past the Palace Hotel and up the slope. You'll see the jail house on your left."

Sears nodded once, then turned his attention to Molly. "You still haven't told me what you're doing here."

Molly had no intention of answering as she returned his cold stare, but the silence was broken by Winfield Shaw.

"Miss Owens works for me, marshal," he said.

Sears grunted, then turned and motioned for the other marshals to follow him as he stepped off the loading platform and strode toward Bennett.

"I get the feeling he doesn't much like you," Shaw said.

Molly rode beside him in the buggy to his office above the Cripple Creek Bank. Shaw asked a few tactful questions about her acquaintance with Joe Sears, but Molly answered vaguely, not telling him of the marshal's pursuit and killing of Charley Castle. Shaw did not press his questions.

A quarter of an hour after they came into the office, Clint walked in the door. He told Shaw that he had reserved the entire third floor of the Imperial Hotel even though he'd had to buy off half a dozen tenants and bribe the desk clerk to do it.

"Nine marshals?" Clint asked in disbelief when Shaw described his meeting with Joe Sears at the train station. "We need a larger force than that, Win."

"What we've got is a sawed-off U.S. marshal who thinks he's a larger force," Shaw said. Turning to Molly, he asked, "Will Sears do as he says, or is he all talk?"

"He'll jump in with both feet," Molly said.

Shaw looked at Clint. "Well, maybe Sears will buy time for us. Both the miners and strikebreakers will think twice before doing battle with U.S. marshals. Any idea when the Colorado Militia will be ready to move?"

Clint shrugged. "A couple days, a couple weeks, I don't know."

"I'll telegraph another message to the governor," Shaw said, "and remind him of our situation down here. Maybe Sears will keep the lid on for two or three days." He added, "I wish that little rooster luck."

Molly was right in her prediction that Marshal Joe Sears would jump into the fray with both feet. Word spread through the saloons on Myers Avenue late in the afternoon that Sears had run down Riley Newcomb and arrested him on charges of inciting to riot and damaging property on the American Eagle Mine claim.

Newcomb was locked up in a cell in the

Cripple Creek jail, and by the time Molly got there, a crowd of miners had gathered on the street in front of the red brick building. The men were angry.

"Set Riley loose!"

"We'll come in after him!"

"The damned strikebusters are the ones who oughta be in jail!"

Molly stood at the edge of the crowd and listened to the miners' shouts. Then she saw them swarm to the double front doors of the building and push against them, yelling curses and demanding that Riley Newcomb be freed. The big doors, covered with sheet iron, were barred from the inside and did not budge.

Still the men pressed forward, venting their rage as their voices swelled in a rising crescendo of shouts until behind them, from across Bennett, came a gunshot.

Molly jumped, as she was startled by the loud report. Like the miners, she quickly turned around. A line of nine horsemen was there, facing the crowd. The man in the middle, holding his revolver in the air, was Joe Sears. The other marshals sat in their saddles with rifles braced on their right thighs, barrels slanting upward.

"You men disperse," Sears said. "You've made your point. Now go home."

"We ain't leaving until Newcomb's out!" shouted a bearded miner.

Another man yelled, "Who the hell are you, mister?"

Sears said, "United States Marshal Joe Sears." He nodded to the horsebackers on either side of him. "These men are all U.S. marshals, and we're ordering you to disperse — right now."

"How much are the mine owners paying you?" a man shouted.

"The taxpayers pay me to keep the peace," Sears said. "If I have to lock up every man on this street to get the job done, I'll do it."

A tense silence followed. Molly looked at the miners, wondering if they would call Sears' bluff. She estimated the crowd to be well over a hundred men, and nine marshals arresting all of them made an unlikely prospect.

But these men were without a leader. The tension was broken when several moved away from the doors, and the others slowly followed. Molly turned to walk with them back to Myers but stopped when her name was called. She turned and saw Joe Sears rein his horse toward her.

He drew up and looked down at her. The brim of his Stetson shaded his wide forehead and eyes. "Stay clear of me, woman."

"The pleasure will be mine, marshal," Molly said.

He studied her. "You've got a way of turning up at the wrong place at the wrong time. I've got my hands full without having to work around you. Stick your nose in where it doesn't belong and I'll put you behind bars so fast your head'll spin." He added, "Like I did in Denver."

"I guess I should thank you for not gunning me down," Molly said, clenching her jaw against her rising anger.

"Don't get mouthy," Sears said. "I never wanted to shoot Castle. I thought he was going for his gun."

"You're telling that lie to the wrong person," Molly said. "I know better. I was there. Remember?"

"You think he wasn't reaching for his gun," Sears said, "just like I think he was. Who's right?"

"No man would draw on a dozen men who had taken aim at him," Molly said. "You never gave him a chance to surrender."

"He had plenty of chances," Sears said, "but he kept running."

"And that's what made you mad enough to gun him down, wasn't it?" Molly asked.

"Hell, there's no use in talking to you about it," Sears said. "It was all for nothing, anyhow."

Molly stared at him. "What are you saying?"

Sears did not answer but started to turn his horse.

Molly grasped a rein, holding on when the horse tossed his head. "Tell me!"

Sears shrugged. "Ain't much to tell. We arrested a man for killing that whore in Bluebell. Castle was running for nothing."

Molly's eyes filled with tears. "You bastard," she whispered. "You bastard."

Sears jerked the horse away and rode off.

CHAPTER XXVII

Molly stood on the edge of Bennett in the shadow of the two-story jail house, and she shook with rage and sorrow. Her eyes flooded with tears, and through those tears she watched Joe Sears ride away.

She brought a handkerchief out of her handbag and wiped her eyes and cheeks. Movement caught her eye. Turning, she saw the large double doors of the jail house ease open.

Broyles stepped outside and waved at Sears and the marshals. Joe Sears veered across the street. The two men consulted for a moment and then Sears rode away, leading his party down the street.

Molly saw someone in the doorway behind the city marshal, and a second man stepped outside, carrying a double-barreled shotgun. He was Clint Lange.

Surprised, Molly stared. Then she took a deep breath. An idea came to her. She composed herself as well as she could and walked toward the two men.

"I want to see Riley Newcomb," she said. "Is he here?"

Both Broyles and Clint turned to her, briefly startled by her unexpected appearance.

"Ain't your business to know," Broyles said. When he heard Clint speak her name in a subdued greeting, Broyles asked, "You know her?"

Clint nodded. "Miss Owens works for Win Shaw."

"Now hold on," the city marshal said. "You must have her mixed up with someone else."

"No, I don't," Clint said. "She's an investigator who's doing undercover work for Win."

"Well, I'll be damned," Broyles said, turning to stare at Molly. "You know, I kinda figured you weren't who you claimed to be."

Molly realized Clint had revealed her identity for a purpose. Once word got around about her, she would not be an effective investigator. Clint wanted to make certain she would be unable to function as one.

"That's right," Molly said, thinking quickly. "I work for the Fenton Investigative Agency. I believe I can help you find out what the miners plan to do next — if you'll let me."

Broyles' bulldog face remained impassive as he eyed her. "How so?"

"By talking to Newcomb," Molly said. "He trusts me. Doesn't he, Clint?"

Clint acknowledged the point with a brief nod.

"We'd better step into my office," Broyles said, "and have us a talk."

Molly walked with them into the building. The main floor, a high-ceilinged room, was lighted by large windows covered with heavy screens. Along one wall were barred detention cells, and on the opposite wall Molly saw a police desk manned by a uniformed deputy.

Straight ahead was an office with the door standing open. Molly followed Broyles into it, and Clint came in after her.

Broyles closed the door. He took the shotgun from Clint and put it into a rack on the wall that held half a dozen other weapons. Moving around his desk, the big lawman gestured to a pair of captain's chairs as he sat down.

"Now I want to know what you've been doing in my town, Miss Owens," he said.

Molly described the investigation she had

conducted for Winfield Shaw, beginning with her interview with Candace Smith and concluding with her work as go-between for Shaw and Riley Newcomb. All of this was confirmed by Clint, who listened with a grim expression on his face, as though he realized his plan was backfiring. Broyles clearly regarded Molly with new respect.

"So that's how Luckett fits into this thing," he said, referring to her original assignment that brought her to Cripple Creek. "You still figure he murdered that woman?"

Molly nodded.

"Can you prove it?" Broyles asked.

She sensed in his tone of voice that he had revised his opinion of Luckett. A lot of other people had too, Molly guessed, since Luckett brought a force of lawless thugs to town.

"Not yet," Molly replied.

"Not yet," Broyles repeated flatly. "You know, Miss Owens, we'll get along a whole lot better if you tell me everything you know."

"I can't," Molly said, "without incriminating myself."

"Trust me to look out for your best interests," Broyles said. "Now tell me what you know."

Molly did trust him. He wasn't a particularly intelligent man, but he was straightforward.

"Luckett has an engagement ring in his safe," Molly said, "that belonged to Candace. She was wearing it the last time I talked to her. The ring was special to her, and I have no doubt that she died wearing it."

"And her murderer stole it," Broyles concluded. He regarded her. "So you cracked Luckett's safe, did you?"

"I'm not going to admit that," Molly said with a smile.

Broyles leaned back in his chair. "I'd like to find Luckett and hold him for a few days. Sears and I want to put the leaders of this dispute, all of them, behind bars. But that diamond ring isn't quite enough to bring down a murder charge."

"Will you let me talk to Newcomb?" Molly said.

"If I do, I'll expect you to tell me everything he says," Broyles said.

"I won't withhold —" Molly began.

Clint stood and said abruptly, "Newcomb isn't going to talk. He's not stupid."

Broyles looked up at him. "You said yourself that he trusts Miss Owens. Maybe he wants to send a message to Shaw."

"This is a waste of time," Clint said. "He won't talk."

"We won't know until we try," Molly said.

"That's what I figure, too," Broyles said slowly, watching Clint pace back and forth. "Something wrong, Clint?"

"No, no," Clint replied. He added. "We don't have much time, and right now we're wasting time."

"This won't take long," Broyles said. "And if Miss Owens here can get some idea what the miners plan to do next —"

Clint slapped his hands together and turned away, but he said nothing.

Broyles stood. "This way," he said to Molly. Outside the office, he said, "Clint's jumpy, ain't he?"

Molly soon found out why. She followed Marshal Broyles up a flight of iron stairs. At the landing, he unlocked an armored door, locked it behind Molly, and led the way down an aisle between two rows of barred cells.

Catcalls greeted Molly until Broyles uttered a terse order that silenced the prisoners. They lay stretched out on steel bunks, and farther down the line Molly saw two men playing checkers through the bars. They stopped their game and stared as Molly passed by.

The end cell, surrounded by empty ones, held Riley Newcomb. He sat on the bunk in there, leaning back against the wall, legs crossed in front of him. He looked at Molly but gave no sign of recognition.

Broyles stopped at the door of Newcomb's cell, and in a voice that was appropriately gruff, he said to Molly, "Five minutes, no more."

As the marshal walked away, Newcomb asked, "What do you want?"

"I came here to talk to you," she replied.

"Little late for that, isn't it?" Newcomb asked. He paused and added, "All the talk I heard from you people amounted to so many lies."

"Lies?" Molly said. "I never lied to you."

"Your people had me thrown in here," Newcomb said. "You said I'd be safe."

"You were," Molly said. "You were arrested by Marshal Sears, weren't you? Mr. Shaw didn't have anything to do with having you jailed."

"The hell you say," Newcomb said dully. "Clint Lange takes orders from Shaw, doesn't he?"

Molly moved closer to the cell and grasped the bars. "Tell me what happened."

"Not much to tell," Newcomb said.

"When I left Shaw's cabin, I told him where he could find me. The next thing I know, I'm surrounded by U.S. marshals. Clint Lange was riding with them."

Molly now understood why Clint had not wanted her to see Newcomb. *A senseless act of betrayal* was her first thought, realizing that Shaw must have mentioned to Clint where Riley Newcomb had gone. Clint knew Marshal Sears wanted to lock up the leaders, and he must have decided Newcomb should be the first.

"Clint sometimes acts on his own," Molly said. "I still don't believe Mr. Shaw had anything to do with your arrest."

"Doesn't matter much now, does it?" Newcomb said.

Molly asked, "What's going to happen with the strike?"

Newcomb cast an angry look at her. "How the hell should I know? I don't have any control over those men from this cell."

His implication was clear. The miners were angry, and they were as well organized now as they'd ever been. They might turn to the more violent leaders among them. They were certainly capable of waging war in the district.

The armored door opened at the far end of the cell block, and Broyles came for her.

Molly quickly told Newcomb that she would try to get him released as soon as possible but received only a skeptical glance in reply.

CHAPTER XXVIII

In Broyles' office, with Clint looking on, Molly gave the gist of her conversation with Riley Newcomb to the marshal and explained why she believed the threat of a full-blown labor war was greater with Newcomb in jail than out. She argued for his release.

"That'd be foolish," Clint snapped. "He'd dynamite another mine the minute he got out."

Molly turned to Broyles. The marshal nodded agreement with Clint.

"I reckon Sears has the right idea to put the leaders behind bars until things cool down," he said.

"Those miners won't cool down as long as Newcomb's in jail," Molly said.

Broyles turned his big hands palms up on his desk. "Well, I couldn't let Newcomb out if I wanted to. He's Sears' prisoner."

Molly left the jail house a step behind Clint. On the boardwalk outside, she put her hand on his arm and stopped him.

"Why, Clint?" she asked. "Why did you do it?"

"Do what?" he said, avoiding her eyes.

"Send Sears after Newcomb," she said.

Now Clint looked at her, glaring. "You know why. I told you I'd stop Newcomb and his union scum. They want to bring this country down. Jail is the place for all the union bastards."

"You betrayed Winfield Shaw," Molly said.

Clint pulled away from her and swiftly walked down the boardwalk toward the center of town, his boot heels sounding on the boards like measured drum beats.

Late in the afternoon, Molly answered a knock on the door of her room in the Old Homestead. She found Winfield Shaw standing in the hall, holding his hat in both hands before him. In a subdued voice, he asked if he could come in.

"Of course," Molly said.

"I understand you saw Clint in Broyles' office," he said as he entered.

Molly nodded and showed him to the settee.

"Clint and I had a long talk," Shaw said, sitting down. "Seems like we don't agree on much anymore. He admitted he'd broken the trust you and I had established with

Newcomb and defended himself by explaining his political ideas — passionately."

Shaw paused, looking tired and old. He drew a breath. "Well, the upshot is that Clint will no longer act on my behalf."

Molly understood what he meant, but she could hardly believe it. "You released him?"

Shaw nodded. "I sent him packing." The millionaire seemed to sag as he spoke. He looked at Molly and added, "I need you now more than ever, Miss Owens."

"My effectiveness as an investigator may be limited," she said, and went on to tell how Clint had revealed her role to Marshal Broyles.

"Seems Clint is quick to betray his friends these days," Shaw mused. "Well, at this point, it may not matter if folks know who you are. See what you can find out about the miners."

"Where do you want me to start?" she asked.

"Rumor has it that the strikebreakers plan to run the miners off the El Paso and Jackpot properties," Shaw said. "When, I don't know. I've wired the governor that the situation is critical down here, so maybe he'll put a spur to the militia."

"What does Marshal Sears have in mind?" Molly asked.

"That little rooster would only tell me what he's telling everyone else — that he'll have every lawbreaker behind bars in a matter of hours," he said. "As a result, no one's seen Lucky or the strikebreakers for the last day or so. And the miners are madder than ever. Everyone's on a short fuse."

"And Sears is making sparks," Molly said.

An hour before sundown, Molly rode the gelding up the slope of Myers Avenue toward the ore-wagon road that led to Gold Hill. She wanted to find out exactly where the El Paso and Jackpot mines were and possibly get some idea of the miners' fortifications, if any. Shaw could use that information.

She knew the general location of the two mines from various conversations she'd overheard since her arrival in Cripple Creek. They were adjacent claims on the east slope of Gold Hill. Both had been shut down and occupied by striking miners since the day Riley Newcomb had called the strike.

As she rode up to the far end of Myers, passing through the slum outskirts of town, she reflected on her conversation with Shaw and wondered if Luckett was in hiding or had left the district.

The frame and tarpaper-shack cribs there lined the street like ramshackle structures built by a mad carpenter. Molly saw the crib where Candace had lived. The door with the stained-glass window was closed.

Molly's gaze went to the crib next door. Smoke drifted out of the stovepipe punching through the patchwork roof. Molly eased back on the reins as she rode past, then turned the horse and guided him across the street to the crib where the fat woman lived.

The crib door opened after Molly's knock, and a small gust of perfumed air, tinged with the odor of coal smoke, came out. The fat woman stepped into the aperture.

"Yes?" she said.

Molly saw a glint of recognition in the woman's eyes. A large woman with a petite voice, she wore a heavy red dress with lace trim at the neck and sleeves, bright rouge on her cheeks, and her strawberry-blonde hair was combed out, ready for an evening's work.

"I spoke to you after Candace's death," Molly said. The fat woman looked at Molly but gave no sign that she remembered.

"You saw Leroy Luckett that day, didn't

you?" Molly asked.

"I don't know what you're talking about," she said.

Molly smiled. "You don't have to answer to me. I only wanted to help you if I can."

"How . . . how can you help me?" she asked in a tiny voice.

"Marshal Broyles and a federal marshal named Sears are after Luckett," Molly said. "One of those lawmen will be coming here to talk to you. I thought you should know so you can have your story ready."

"Story," the fat woman repeated.

"You won't have to fear anything from Luckett after they bring him in," Molly said. She met the woman's steady gaze. This was a cat-and-mouse game, and Molly wondered if the mouse felt cornered.

"I don't know what you're talking about," the fat woman said. She looked downward.

"I understand," Molly said, backing away a step. "You have to be careful. If you need help, you can find me in the Old Homestead. Ask for Molly." She turned and went to her horse, hoping the woman would call her back and admit that she had seen Luckett that day.

But she didn't. Molly reached the horse, put her foot in the stirrup, and swung up. As she rode away, she glanced back and saw

238

that the fat woman had retreated into the crib and closed the door.

The bluff had failed, and now the best Molly could hope for was that the woman would turn to her later, if she actually had seen Luckett leave Candace's crib through the back door that day. If she had, then she knew Luckett was a murderer, and she would be guided by fear. Tomorrow, Molly planned to reveal her suspicions to Broyles. Perhaps a visit to the crib by him would bring out the truth.

Just before sundown, Molly followed the ore-wagon road up the slope of Gold Hill, and when she reached a fork in the road, she turned east, taking the opposite branch from the one that led to the Independence. Half a mile farther, she left that road and urged the horse straight uphill through a break in the pines.

Glancing over her shoulder, she saw that the sky over the western horizon had turned fiery red as the sun sank below the jagged line of mountain peaks. A few minutes later, she looked back again and saw that the red had become pink. This delicate color lingered for a time, but when Molly reached the crest of Gold Hill, the sky was pale blue, and the air was rapidly turning cold.

The top of Gold Hill was open ground

here, too, as it was on the other end near the American Eagle Mine. Ahead, the land sloped downward toward a thick stand of brush edged by scrubby pines. The trees were twisted and gnarled by wind and harsh weather. The altitude here, Molly judged, was about 11,000 feet.

Somewhere beyond those dwarfed pines, farther down the hillside, she expected to find the El Paso and Jackpot mines. She looked intently for mine buildings or head frames, not realizing until too late why the gelding suddenly tossed his head.

"Stop right there, lady."

Kneeling in the twisted trees off to her right a dozen yards was a man aiming a long-barreled Springfield rifle at her.

CHAPTER XXIX

"Get off that horse," he ordered.

The man was no miner. He wore clean clothes, shiny boots, and a Stetson. Around his waist were two revolvers and a full cartridge belt. Beard stubble darkened his jaw.

"I beg your pardon," Molly said, hoping she sounded properly indignant. "Is it money you want? You don't look like a common road agent."

"I'm not after your damned money," he said. "Now, get off that horse."

"And you'll shoot me if I don't?" Molly demanded. "A lady can't even take an evening ride without being molested —"

Exasperated, the man got to his feet and strode to her, switching his rifle to his left hand while grasping the horse's reins at the bit with his right.

"Now do as I told you, lady, and climb off the goddamned horse."

Molly placed one hand on the saddle horn

and leaned forward as though dismounting, but with her other hand she reached under her jacket and drew her revolver.

The man's face stretched in amazement as he stared into the gun barrel inches from his nose.

"Drop the rifle," Molly said. When the man hesitated, she said, "Drop it, or I'll shoot you where you stand."

The man swallowed and obeyed.

"Now unbuckle your gun belt and back away," Molly said. She watched him unhook the buckle of his cartridge belt. He let the revolvers fall to his feet and stepped back two paces.

Molly dismounted. She took the rope hanging from her saddle and backed the man into the dwarfed pine trees.

"What . . . what you gonna do?" he asked.

"See that little tree over there?" Molly asked, motioning with her gun to a gnarled pine four feet in height. "Sit down against the trunk and cross your wrists behind it."

Molly moved around him as the man slowly sat down with his back to the tree. She knelt behind him and slipped a loop over his outstretched wrists, drew it tight, and knotted it. Wrapping the rope around the trunk, she tied it again.

"I thought you said you was a lady," the man said.

"You'd better hope I am," Molly said, stepping in front of him. "Who do you work for?"

He looked up at her but did not reply.

Molly stooped down and aimed the revolver at his knee. "Mister, I don't have much time. Talk fast, or suffer the consequences."

"You wouldn't shoot me," he growled.

"I won't kill you," Molly said. "But I'm in a hurry, and I will maim you if you don't tell me what I want to know." She cocked the revolver.

The man's jaw quivered. "My god, no!"

"Who do you work for?" Molly asked.

"Lucky," he whispered. "I work for Leroy Luckett."

"Where is he now?" Molly asked.

The man drew a sharp breath as Molly pressed the gun barrel against the side of his knee. "Down there," he said jerking his head toward the sloping hillside.

"Don't make me pry every detail out of you," Molly said. "Down where?"

"We took over the El Paso," he said. "Ran the strikers out and took it over. Now they're holed up in the Jackpot."

"You're in a standoff with them?" Molly asked.

He nodded. "For now."

Molly stood. She turned and looked down slope. The miners had probably given up the El Paso easily and fallen back to the Jackpot. One mine was easier to defend than two. Now the strikebreakers must be planning a way to dislodge the miners and would likely put the plan into action early in the morning. Other guards were probably out here to keep the U.S. marshals from surprising the main party of strikebreakers.

Molly left the man bound to the tree. She took his guns and led her horse several yards down slope, moving cautiously.

The stunted trees gave way to a stretch of open ground. Farther down the hillside was a boulder field, and beyond it Molly saw a forest of tall pines mixed with aspen trees. Over the tree tops was a head frame.

She left her horse behind along with the guard's guns. Slinging her handbag and field glasses over her shoulder, she sprinted across the open ground to the boulder field.

The boulders, rounded and cracked chunks of gray granite, were the size of wagon wheels and larger. They provided good cover. Molly wanted to get closer to the El Paso Mine to find out how large a force of men was there. To her advantage, the light was growing thin. She would not be seen from the mine buildings, and she could leave under the cover of darkness.

Making her way through the maze of boulders, Molly saw angular, steep-roofed buildings ahead. They were among stumps where the pines had been felled for mine timbering. Molly skirted one huge boulder and stopped behind another. Looking over it, she now saw lamplight in the window of one building.

She took the field glasses out of the case and raised them to her eyes. The yellow glowing window came into focus. A moment later, she felt hard steel punch into her back.

"Now just what the hell are you doing here?"

Immediately recognizing the voice, Molly lowered the field glasses and turned. She faced the man who had abducted her and taken her to the cabin where Luckett had tried to assault her.

"Where's your mask?" she asked. He was a long-faced man with pale eyes and a thin nose.

He prodded her with the barrel of the Winchester in his hands. "Move on down the hill since you're so damned curious to know what's going on down there. I know a man who wants to have a long talk with you." He added, "And there's plenty of other men who'll take their turn."

Molly did not move for a moment.

"Don't make me mess up that pretty face," he said. Molly turned and strode down the hill. The strikebreaker prodded her through the weathered stumps of pine trees toward the largest building where the window glowed with lamplight.

She glanced around at the other buildings, looked up at the towering head frame, and saw ore buckets on thick cables. Beyond the base of the head frame were massive piles of rock and soil that had been drilled, blasted, hammered, and lifted by steam power out of the underground tunnels.

They were seen. The side door of the building swung open, sending a wide ray of light on to the darkening ground. A tall man moved into the doorway. He was back lighted, and Molly did not recognize him until she was a dozen paces away.

"Well, look who's here," Leroy Luckett said. He stepped out of the doorway and put his bowler hat on his head.

"Found her in the rocks up yonder," the long-faced man said. "She got past Bob somehow."

"Better go back there and see what she

did to him," Luckett said.

"All right." He paused. "I never looked her over for a sneak gun, Lucky. She had one last time."

"My pleasure," Luckett said with a grin. He came closer.

With the rifle barrel jammed in her back, Molly stood still while Luckett bent down and lifted her divided skirt to her thighs. He ran his hands up her legs, then moved his groping hands outside her clothes to her breasts. He paused a moment, looking into her eyes. He slid his hands under her jacket and came out with her revolver.

"Well, well," he said, examining the nickel-plated revolver. He aimed it at her. "Now tell me, just who the hell are you?"

"Molly Owens," she replied.

"Another smart answer like that will get you a piece of hot lead," he said, taking deliberate aim.

Molly met his gaze. "I'm an operative for the Fenton Investigative Agency."

Luckett's face darkened with anger. "I should have guessed — damned if I shouldn't have figured that out. Shaw hired you, didn't he?"

Molly did not reply. She heard a *click* as Luckett thumbed back the hammer of her revolver.

"If you're going to kill me," she said, "get it over with. I won't tell you who I'm working for or anything else."

"The hell you say," Luckett said. He stared into her eyes a moment, then slowly lowered the gun. "I know as much as I need to know. Shaw's been out to get me for a long time —"

"You've got that backwards, don't you?" Molly asked, thinking that she had nothing to lose now. "You were out to get him. You tried to use Candace Smith to get him."

"I was trying to get back some of the fortune due me," he said, his voice rising. "Shaw robbed me out of a mine that made over half a million dollars. He liquored me up and paid a fraction of what it was worth."

"But no one knew how much it was worth at the time," Molly said.

Luckett's pent-up anger boiled over. He drew back his fist and threw a looping punch. Molly tried to duck back, but was stopped by the strikebreaker who jammed a rifle in her back.

Luckett's fist slammed into her jaw. Molly felt her knees weaken, but she stayed on her feet. Half turning, she grasped the rifle barrel with one hand and slugged the strikebreaker in the throat with the other.

Her ears ringing, she whirled to face

Luckett. His eyes were stretched open in surprise as he watched the strikebreaker sink to his knees, clutching his neck and gasping for air.

Molly grasped Luckett's wrist, raised his arm and stepped under it, and gave it a downward thrust. His feet came off the ground as he spun around in midair, landing on his back.

Three men came running out of the mine building, brandishing guns. One shouted at Molly to raise her hands. She slowly obeyed, and watched Luckett raise up to all fours as the men stopped a few feet away.

"You all right, Lucky?" one asked.

He nodded and stood, glaring at Molly. "Business before pleasure, Miss Owens. I'll save you for later." He motioned toward the head frame. "Over there. Move it."

Molly turned toward the steel-screened cage poised over the mine shaft at the base of the head frame. Luckett shoved her and she stumbled toward it. One of the strike-breakers moved ahead of them and opened the gate to the cage. Luckett pushed her inside. "I'll lower you to the first level," he said, "where you'll have company."

Molly slumped down on the cold metal floor of the cage, looking out as the gate was closed.

The steel cage sank slowly into the darkness, down into air that was cold and damp. She heard water dripping, drops steadily plinking into a pool somewhere far below. Presently, the cage stopped, and Molly sat up.

The ringing in her ears had stopped, but she felt sleepy tired from Luckett's punch. Surrounded by blackness deep in this mine, she could not see her hand in front of her face. She listened to the dripping water, and then a new sound reached her.

Molly slowly stood in the cage, feeling the screened sides. She saw nothing, but the sound came again, a pained moan as though an injured animal was waiting for her in the darkness. She turned toward the sound.

Her head had cleared somewhat, and she felt stronger. Opening the cage gate, she stuck her foot out, feeling for something solid with the toe of her boot. She heard the moan again.

Her foot touched ground. Reaching out with one hand, she touched a timbered wall. A tunnel stretched out before her.

"Who's there?" Molly asked. No reply came. She repeated, "Who's there?"

This time her question was answered by a moan. Stepping out of the cage, Molly edged forward, feeling as though she was walking into eternity. Having no way of knowing if another deep shaft yawned before her, she took each step with great care.

Four steps away from the cage, her foot nudged something bulky. She slowly knelt and reached down into the blackness. Her fingertips touched fabric, a man's coat.

The man lay crumpled before her. Molly felt his body. His legs were drawn up against his chest, like a child asleep. She touched his face, and her fingers came away sticky. He moaned again. This man had been severely beaten.

Molly thought a moment, then grasped the man under the arms and dragged him back toward the cage. She was uncertain what would happen but decided she would be better off there in case the cage was hoisted to the surface. She would rather face the dangers up there than be left down here.

The man was thick bodied and heavy. Molly dragged him an inch at a time. She planted her feet and pulled, then stepped back and did it again, leaning back and pulling with all her strength.

She finally dragged him to the cage and pulled him inside. She lifted his legs in and closed the gate. Suddenly tired, she slumped down on the cold steel floor beside him, listening to his shallow breathing and occasional moans.

After resting, Molly searched the man's pockets. She found nothing but a sack of tobacco and package of cigarette papers. Then, in a vest pocket, she found a box of matches.

Striking one, Molly blinked against the sudden flash of bright light. She held the flaming match closer to the man, drawing it toward his face. He was Joe Sears.

CHAPTER XXX

The night was the longest of her life, with every second ticked off by the brittle sounds of water dripping deep in the mine shaft below the cage. The air was chilly and wet smelling, black as tar, and Molly sat huddled beside Sears on the cold metal floor, waiting.

At dawn, faint light filtered into the cage. Molly looked up through the metal screen overhead and saw the greased pulleys and cables leading to the head frame far above ground. Minutes later, she heard the distant popping of gunfire.

Sears roused. He grimaced when he tried to straighten his legs out. Molly gave him as much room as she could in the cramped cage, and now, by the dim light of morning, she clearly saw his battered face. His nose was bent to the side, and one eye was swollen shut. The other blinked and opened, moving until it found her.

Sears' swollen lips quivered, but no words

came from his mouth. He groaned as he tried to raise up. Molly grasped his shoulders and helped him sit.

Joe Sears slumped against the far corner of the cage, leaning his head back as he stared at Molly through his good eye.

She asked, "What happened?"

"Trick . . . a trick," Sears said hoarsely. Blood oozed from the corner of his mouth. "Luckett sent word . . . turn himself in . . . meet me . . . alone . . ."

"He beat you?" Molly asked.

Even in this battered and weakened condition, Sears managed to shake his head indignantly. "Three . . . took three of the bastards . . ."

Stacatto sounds of gunfire and booms of shotguns came steadily now. Sears revived. Groaning against pain in his ribs, he managed to stand. He tried to look up, then hunched over and leaned back, resting a hip on the screened wall of the cage. He looked down at Molly.

"Never thought . . . we'd end up . . . this way," he said. "Reckon . . . you got . . . nothing but hate . . . for me."

Molly replied with a shake of her head. Strangely, she felt no rage toward this man. She could no longer hate him for killing Charley Castle. But at the same time, she felt little compassion for him as a wounded man. He was a man of violence, and the public threats he'd made about throwing Luckett behind bars had been answered by violence.

A series of explosions shook the ground, followed by stillness. Molly stood in the cage, guessing that the miners had fought the well-armed strikebreakers as long as they could, then had dynamited the Jackpot and retreated.

As Molly looked up at the screened ceiling of the cage, a vivid memory shot into her mind. The day she had first ridden to the Independence Mine with her plan to help Candace Smith leave Cripple Creek, she'd seen Winfield Shaw and several mechanics working on the hoist. Now she remembered seeing one of the men raise and lower the cage several inches by turning a large crank.

And last night Luckett had lowered the cage without starting up the mine's steam engine.

Of course! Molly thought as she examined the section of metal screen that comprised the ceiling of the cage. *The hoist can be operated manually.* Otherwise, miners would be trapped down here if the steam engine ever failed.

The heavy screen on top of the cage was to protect miners from falling rocks, Molly realized, and now she saw how to remove it. She pulled out four steel pins, one at each corner, and the ceiling came loose.

"What . . . doing?" Sears asked in a muffled voice.

Molly did not reply. She set the section of screen down and looked up at the pulleys. A crank was there, secured by straps. She unhooked them, and the cold metal of the big crank came into her hands.

Inserting the end of it into the hole of a cogged gear, she pulled. The crank moved with surprising ease, and the cage raised up a few inches. Sears swore excitedly.

Every revolution of the crank raised the cage a foot or more. Molly turned it until she grew arm weary, and then Sears took a turn, groaning against the pain of injured ribs.

More gunshots reached Molly's ears as the light in the cage became brighter. When Sears tired, she took another turn, looking up at the rectangle of blue sky overhead. It became larger and larger, and less than half an hour after she'd discovered the way to escape, the cage reached the surface.

She opened the gate and helped Sears hobble out. Hearing running horses and shouts, mixed with scattered gunshots, she saw Sears turn in that direction.

"My men," he said.

Minutes later, a pair of U.S. marshals came riding through the trees at a gallop. They were followed by a third horsebacker — Clint Lange.

The men reined up when they reached Molly and Joe Sears. The marshals stared in shocked silence at the beaten man. Clint dismounted and came to Molly.

"Are you all right?" he asked.

Molly nodded.

He looked at her critically. "That's quite a bruise on your jaw."

Molly gingerly touched the soreness there. "I took my eyes off Luckett at the wrong moment," she said. "Did you get him?"

Clint shook his head. "We rounded up most of the strikebreakers, but Luckett got away. He's probably headed for the state border by now."

Sears swore. He looked up at the marshals and spoke through swollen lips. "Get him."

After the capture of the strikebreakers was complete, Molly found her handbag and field glasses in one of the mine buildings. She then searched through a pile of confiscated guns and found both her revolver and the derringer that had been taken from her the day she was abducted by the masked riders. Evidently, the long-faced man was one of the captured strikebreakers.

Among the horses tied to the rail near one of the mine buildings was her gelding. She found the animal to be all right and led him to a nearby trough. A few minutes later, Clint joined her there and watered his horse.

While the horses noisily drank, Clint seemed to search for words. He crossed his arms over his chest, looked down at the ground, then at the horses, and then at Molly.

"Some of the marshals will march the prisoners back to Cripple Creek," he said at last. "The others are riding after Luckett. I'll go with them." He paused. "Leroy Luckett stood to make a fortune today."

"How?" Molly asked.

"If he'd been successful in driving the strikers off these two mine properties," Clint said, "he would have been paid in shares of mining stock — $100,000 worth."

Molly looked at him in surprise.

"I know," Clint went on, "because the mine owners made the same offer to me when they found out I'd left Shaw."

"But you turned them down," Molly said.

Clint nodded. "I told them the law was on their side, and they should use it to assert their property rights. Their view was that it would take months to win the case in court, compared to a quick show of force that would scare every union man out of the district."

A marshal called out to Clint. He turned and waved that he was coming. But he did not move away immediately. He turned back and cast a lingering look at Molly.

"I'm sorry," he said, "sorry our trails parted."

Molly met his gaze. "I am, too."

"We had something good between us," he said.

Molly nodded.

"I guess we both did what we had to do," Clint said. "I know I did. I have no regrets about that."

But even as he spoke, Molly knew that he lied, or he wasn't being truthful with himself. He had betrayed Winfield Shaw, and he'd betrayed her.

Clint's name was called again, with more urgency this time, and he abruptly turned away and strode to the waiting marshals.

Molly left soon afterward. She rode along the winding ore-wagon road and came in sight of Cripple Creek just as the sun was rising over the eastern horizon. Much had happened since last night's sunset, she thought, looking toward the snowy mountains far to the west. Last night, those peaks had been purple as plums. Now, touched by morning sunlight, they were the color of roses.

After descending the hill into Cripple Creek, Molly turned on First Street. Halfway down the block, an idea came to her. She turned the horse, guiding him into a narrow alley behind the saloons and gambling parlors on Myers.

She looked ahead at the rear of the Gold Coin Club, and her suspicion was confirmed. The back door stood open.

Molly reined up and stepped down out of the saddle. Climbing the short staircase to the stoop, she drew her revolver from her shoulder holster. She edged into the back hallway, peering into the shadows. No one was there.

Molly walked silently down the hall to Luckett's office. That door stood open, too. Moving into the doorway, she halted as she caught the faint odor of coal oil.

The room was empty. Lighted only by morning light streaming in from the hall, Molly realized that the lamp on Luckett's desk had been extinguished not long ago.

She stepped in, seeing the open safe in the far corner of the room. She moved around the leather upholstered chairs grouped around the low table and went to Luckett's desk. She touched the glass chimney of the lamp with her fingertips. The glass was still hot. Luckett had needed the light to open his safe by the combination.

Molly left the club and led her horse out of the back alley and crossed Myers to the Old Homestead. Her muscles ached from sitting on the cold steel floor of the cage all night, and now she thought ahead to a steaming hot bath.

The thought should have relaxed her, but it did not. Her part in this case was finished, but she took little satisfaction from it. She found no comfort in the knowledge that Luckett would eventually be caught. Joe Sears would run him down no matter how long it took.

As she tied the gelding to the hitching post in front of the Old Homestead, Molly saw a brief flurry of activity behind the window of the front parlor. A moment later, the door opened, and Pearl leaned out.

"Someone's here to see you." She wore a flowing robe of silk over her nightgown.

From her urgent manner and the distraught expression on her face, Molly realized something was amiss. She hurried into the entryway and was about to ask what had happened when she looked into the front parlor.

Standing just inside was the fat woman who lived in the crib next door to Candace. She clutched a bundle to her breasts. "You're an investigator, aren't you?"

Molly nodded and cast an inquiring glance at Pearl. "Win told me your secret was out," she said, "and when Sharon came here asking how you could help her, I told her who you worked for."

"I'll help you any way I can, Sharon," Molly said.

In a voice barely louder than a whisper, she said, "You were right about Lucky. And you were right about me. I lied to you because I was scared. I saw Lucky run out the back door of Candace's crib that morning, and when I found her, I knew he'd done it." She swallowed. "But I couldn't prove it, and who'd take my word against his? If I accused him — well, I was afraid, afraid I'd be next."

Pearl said, "You had Lucky figured from the start, Molly. I thought I knew the man, but he had me fooled. Me and plenty of others in this town." To Sharon, she said impatiently, "Well, go on, girl, tell her."

"This morning, Lucky came to my place," she said. "I was scared he was gonna kill me. He probably would have, too, except he needed me. He said he couldn't be seen now and gave me the key to his club. He wrote down the combination to his safe and said he'd give me $100 if I'd bring everything in the safe to him."

Sharon lowered her arms, looking down at the bundle she held wrapped in a light jacket. "I cleaned out his safe, but when I came outside, I saw the Old Homestead. I got to thinking — thinking about what you told me."

After a long pause, Sharon said, "So I never went back to my place. I came straight here and asked for you."

Molly watched in amazement as Sharon opened the jacket in her arms. Inside were all the papers, money, and ore samples from Luckett's safe. Among the papers was the envelope containing several gold rings.

Molly crossed the room to her and took the envelope. She shook out the rings and picked up the tiny diamond ring.

"Recognize this?" she asked Sharon.

Sharon leaned forward and nodded. "That was Candace's. She wore it all the time. The man who gave it to her was her true love. He was going to come back someday."

Molly dropped the rings back into the envelope. "Did Luckett tell you where he was going?"

Sharon shook her head.

"Did he say anything?" Molly asked.

Sharon thought a moment. "All he said was that he had a score to settle, then he was leaving the district."

Molly stared at the fat woman as this information seeped into her mind. Suddenly, she handed the envelope back to her, turned, and hurried toward the door.

"Molly!" Pearl shouted after her. "Where're you off to?"

Molly answered over her shoulder as she yanked the door open. "Shaw's cabin."

CHAPTER XXXI

Molly thrust her boot into the stirrup and swung up into the saddle. Reining the big horse around, she dug in her heels, and the gelding lunged away from the Old Homestead, breaking into a gallop down Myers Avenue.

Molly let the horse run to the edge of town where she turned onto the ore-wagon road that led up the side of Gold Hill. Quickly gaining elevation, she reached a fork in the road and this time took the branch that went to the Independence Mine.

She was filled with a sense of dread, yet at once driven by a compulsion to find out what had happened. She felt certain Luckett had gone to Shaw's cabin after realizing Sharon was not coming back, that she had robbed him.

The irony of that act brought a smile to Molly's lips. Luckett was a user and abuser of women, a man who intimidated women with violence and now one had skinned him.

But the smile was a brief one. Molly had no doubt that he planned to kill Shaw, and by now he'd had time to do it.

A quarter of an hour later, she drew in sight of the side road that angled up slope through the forest to Shaw's cabin. Before reaching it, she reined the horse to a halt and dismounted. She led the gelding off the road a short distance and tied the reins to the white-barked trunk of an aspen tree.

Molly left the horse and climbed uphill through the trees. The aspens gave way to tall pines. Fifty yards away, she estimated, was Shaw's cabin in a small grassy clearing.

The forest floor was carpeted with pine needles. Molly walked silently through the trees until she caught sight of the log cabin. She hesitated, then moved to her right, staying well back in the trees while peering through the branches at the clearing. A saddle horse was there, grazing.

Then Molly saw a body. She edged closer to the tree line for a better look. Sprawled on the ground was the corpse of a man wearing a flannel shirt and denim trousers. A shotgun lay on the ground beside him.

The body was neither Shaw's nor

Luckett's. Molly saw a dark bullet hole in his cheek below one eye and recognized him as the man who guarded Shaw's cabin, the man who had driven her there in the buggy for her first meeting with Winfield Shaw.

A shot sounded from within the cabin. Startled, Molly dashed through the trees away from the front of the cabin. The side she approached was windowless, and when she was completely out of sight of the open front door, she sprinted out of the trees to the log wall.

She leaned against the solid wall, hearing no sound but her own quickened breathing. Edging around the front of the cabin, she peered past the protruding ends of the peeled logs. The grazing horse ignored her, and in the treetops birds chirped. They were silenced by another gunshot from inside the cabin.

Molly moved quickly around the corner. Hugging the wall, she advanced to the open door, holding her revolver at the ready. She stopped at the edge of the doorjamb, and listened.

A voice droned inside the cabin. She could not hear words, but she recognized the deep voice of Leroy Luckett.

Molly inched forward, looking into the dim interior of the cabin. Luckett stood with his back to her, under the chandelier. He held a revolver trained on Winfield Shaw.

The millionaire stood beside the dining table, clutching the back of a chair for support. He was bleeding from both arms.

Now Molly heard Luckett's words.

"Ruined me . . . rich bastard . . . never should have . . ."

She stepped into the doorway and took aim. Luckett had shot to maim Shaw, and probably intended to slowly kill him.

Before she could order him to drop his gun, Shaw gave her away by looking at her in amazement. Luckett whirled to face her.

"You!" he exclaimed, taking quick aim at her.

Molly dodged as the shot crashed into the doorjamb inches from her ear. She raised her revolver in both hands, aimed, and fired before Luckett could squeeze the trigger again.

The bullet rocked Luckett backward. He tumbled to the carpeted floor, clutching his chest. Molly rushed across the room and snatched the gun from his limp hand.

She looked up at Shaw. His face was drained of color.

"I'm sorry," he said weakly. "I nearly got you killed."

Molly went to him and helped him into the chair. She pulled off his jacket and saw bleeding flesh wounds in both upper arms. "The bullets grazed you," she said.

Shaw stared down at Luckett. "I heard a commotion outside, then a shot. Luckett killed my guard, and busted in here." Shaw paused. "He blames me for everything that went wrong in his life. He came here to kill me."

Molly turned and went to Luckett. She knelt beside him and pressed her fingertips against his neck, feeling for a pulse.

"Is he dead?" Shaw asked.

"Not quite," Molly said. "I'll ride for a doctor."

"Will you come back for the trial?"

The question was asked by Pearl. She stood beside Molly on the loading platform of the train depot. On the tracks behind them a morning freight train had a passenger coach in tow. Departure was a few minutes away.

"I left a written deposition," Molly said. "Sharon's testimony should be enough to convict Luckett. If not, he will certainly be found guilty of murdering Shaw's guard."

Pearl nodded. After a moment she observed, "The doc dug your bullet out of

Lucky to save him for the gallows."

The steam engine's whistle blew shrilly three times, and the last few passengers moved to the steps of the coach.

Molly embraced Pearl. She held the big woman tightly and heard her sob.

"Happy tears," Pearl insisted as she stepped back and touched her eyes with a gloved hand. She blinked rapidly. "I'm proud to have met you, Molly."

"I feel the same way about you," she said.

"You were loyal to Win," Pearl went on in a voice thick with emotion, "and that's why he's alive today."

" 'Board!"

At the conductor's call, Pearl grasped Molly's hands. "You come back sometime. Promise me that."

Molly smiled and squeezed her hands. "I promise." She turned away and climbed aboard the passenger coach. Finding a window seat, she looked out through the wavy glass and saw Pearl raise a hand in a good-by gesture.

Cripple Creek, just a ramshackle town surrounded by mines on the scarred hills, sprawled out behind the woman. Those mines, Winfield Shaw had once said, made fortunes and broke men.

Memories surged through Molly's mind.

Last night French champagne flowed freely during a private celebration in the Old Homestead. She'd said good-by to a grateful Winfield Shaw. His wounds were bandaged and he was in some pain, but had insisted on attending the party. He presented Molly with a bonus of $5,000 and told her that he'd made arrangements to have the buckskin gelding shipped to Denver as a gift for her.

Molly learned from Shaw that a company of state militiamen were at last enroute to Cripple Creek. With the presence of the troopers, and with Shaw's own efforts at peacemaking, further violence might be averted in the mining district.

Shaw had convinced Sears to release Riley Newcomb after charges of destroying property at the American Eagle Mine were dropped. The charges were dropped because Shaw himself had promised to finance the repairs. In return the mine owner agreed to meet with Newcomb. At least some of the combatants would be talking now instead of fighting.

Missing from the party was Clint Lange. Molly learned from Pearl that he'd gone to Colorado Springs where he planned to start a law practice. He had left Cripple Creek without seeing Shaw.

271

Right and wrong were more than matters of law, Molly thought as she looked out the window of the passenger coach, and she believed that deep down Clint knew that to be true. Perhaps he'd admit it to himself one day.

With a sudden rattle of car couplings the coach slid away from the depot. Molly waved to Pearl. While she did want to come back here someday, she did not know when she would be able to take this train ride again. She never knew where her work as a Fenton operative would take her next.

The train wound around the wide curve leading away from Cripple Creek. Molly looked out the window at the picturesque scenery, but already she was thinking ahead. When she arrived back in Denver she would send in her report to Horace Fenton.

Her employer's reply was never long in coming. In a week or ten days a packet would arrive at Mrs. Boatwright's Boarding House for Ladies. The packet would contain background information for a new assignment, and soon Molly would plunge into a new case.